Rebecca Beattie

Somewhere She Is There

Copyright Notice

Dedication

This story is dedicated to my teachers who gave me a
gift more precious than diamonds:

Becky Walsh
Christina Oakley Harrington
David Beattie
David Shephard
Denise Linn
Esther, Jerry and Abraham Hicks
Katherine Beattie
Margaret Beattie
Sally Davies
Tomas D'Aradia
Wayne Dyer

Forward

In 2005, just like Charlotte in *Somewhere She Is There*, I lost my Mother to cancer. The effect for me was simply catastrophic.

In the early days of my grief, I read some of the self-help books that were available on the subject, but none of them offered me much comfort. Several people told me I should try writing letters to my Mum as a way of expressing my grief, and for a long time I did write the letters. However, this conversation just didn't feel right to me, as it felt one-sided and self-absorbed to write letters to which you would not expect a reply.

One day I sat down and wondered what Mum would have said if she had been able to write back to me. And what I wrote was *Somewhere She Is There*.

Prologue

Margaret

My daughter sits across from me on the underground train, wrapped in her own world from head to foot. She doesn't notice the curious glances from her fellow passengers, taking in her unkempt appearance; the clothes that make her look rumpled and frumpy, although usually she is not. She has on a black top, black court shoes and a flowery skirt, which makes her backside look enormous when she walks. She has put on weight, and her hair needs cutting, but somehow I know she no longer has the energy for any of those things, so her hair is drawn back in a tight bun, which only serves to emphasise the new found roundness of her cheeks, and the second chin that she has just recently developed.

The doors hiss open, and a new crowd of people get onto the train, ramming themselves into every available inch of space, stepping on each other's toes, jabbing each other in the back with stray elbows, forcing the people by the door to squash their faces to the glass. There is a sudden burst of laughter from a tourist, caught off-guard by a lurch of the train and the ridiculous position she has been forced to stand in, clinging desperately to the sides of her husband's jacket in a last ditch attempt to not fall out of the doors at the next station. A ripple of unease washes through the carriage at the sudden unexpected noise; they don't like to talk here, and they get unnerved by the sound of someone else talking or laughing, although secretly they all like to listen to other people's conversations and crane their necks slightly to read the newspaper of their neighbouring passengers.

But to all this, my daughter is oblivious. Her face bears the expression of someone who is shell-shocked, traumatised. Her eyes are devoid of any recognition of her surroundings. She is alone in every sense of the word, and the tears start to roll freely down her cheeks, unchecked, unnoticed, so consumed is she in her misery. Not a soul can reach her, and no one here stops to ask, so absorbed are they in their own lives and pretending not to notice the distressed and weeping stray in their midst.

So I sit opposite her, appalled at how grief-stricken she is, and powerless to reach out to her.

I cannot reach her you see, as I am dead.

Part One:
The Dark Flood

One: Charlotte

My mother passed away on New Year's Day in the evening. The only reason I knew the date was because the night before she left me, I lay in the attic bedroom in her house staring up at the stars through the skylight window in the roof. I dozed for a while, but was woken suddenly by a burst of light and colour shooting across the star-lit sky which left me confused, until I realised it was New Years Eve and the rest of the world was celebrating the coming fresh start with champagne and fireworks. All transgressions should be forgiven; all bad habits should be surrendered. Their lives would be given a clean slate for this one night of the year until they awoke the next morning, hung-over and rumpled and realising this was just another day like the last.

The night I saw the fireworks explode across the night sky above me, my mother lay alone and unconscious a few miles away. I did not want this fresh start that life would impose on me any moment now, but neither did I want her to suffer.

In my own naïve way, I held on to my one mantra, "please let her go quickly and not suffer for too long". For what lay beyond her passing I was totally unprepared. All I could think was: "Please let it be quick". I can remember arriving at the hospital one day with my Dad, and he said to me,

"Of course when Mum's fight comes to an end that is when our pain really begins."

At the time I felt almost confused by his comment, as if I couldn't fully grasp the enormity of what he was saying. I almost dismissed the remark out of hand, and yet nothing could have prepared me for the full weight of the devastation that was to sweep through our lives, for those brief weeks we had to pull together and concentrate on her and her alone. I could not allow room for my own feelings, except when I lay awake each night looking up at the dark sky and the stars though the window in the roof. Then I would shake at the thought of what we faced. My limbs would feel cold, and my teeth would chatter, but not because of the temperature of the room. I almost became accustomed to the intense heavy weight in my chest, I almost became accustomed to the way my breath would catch in my throat and my heart would stop momentarily each day. But for her we had to contain this, for my darling Mother we had to push the pause button on all of our fears and feelings and sorrow. For what we faced was only the half of what she faced. I was determined that if she were to walk through the veil between the worlds, we would accompany her as far as we could go.

When faced with the most abject horror, when faced with the most severe suffering imaginable, the human soul contains a staggering, infinite level of strength that I never knew existed before. But considering death and grief is a normal every day part of living, there is surprisingly little help out there when you lose a loved one. There are only those who have lived through it who can share something of the horror they have known, almost like a hidden section of society that whispers the truth quietly when no one is around to hear it. Somewhere in the process I lost at least a year of my life; I have no memory and no recollection of the things that happened in that year. It is as if a great blanket of darkness was thrown over my life, and I doubt if I will ever get it back.

And always I knew that the one person I really needed to turn to for guidance, was the one person I had lost. For the first time in my life, I felt truly alone. I suddenly felt there was an underlying level of anxiety behind everything I felt in life that would never leave me; just like the low hiss of white noise behind sound. I no longer had anyone standing between me and life, no one there to protect me anymore. And the world I saw through these new eyes was one I did not recognise, one I did not want to know. And yet, unless I was to squander the gift of life she had given me, it was one I had to learn to navigate.

But there were no maps here. No satellite navigation tools to see me through. This road was one I had to travel alone.

Two: Charlotte

I always feel as if my mother and I did not get on well when I was a child. I don't think I fitted her expectations, and she would not pander to my adolescent need for high drama. My tears would not take effect, my tantrums would not move her, and yet this made me love her all the more.

I always felt that she favoured my older sister over me. She performed well at school, remained steady through her teenage years, and did not appear to cause the same problems as me. I however was disappointing at school, and was discovered smoking at fifteen, a mere week after I had started. My mother's response was to tell me not to smoke in my room as it made it smell bad, and if I really had to do it, would I mind doing it in the porch?

But later we became closer, when I was old enough to value her no-nonsense steady view of the world, and understand the deep fullness of her compassion. Somehow the storms subsided and we dwelt in warm companionship.

All through my twenties, I was the only person I knew who still holidayed with their family, and this through choice. We had fun together. My relationship with both parents was characterised by lively discussion and irreverent humour. I travelled the world with them and my siblings, and at each destination we would immerse ourselves fully in the local culture, emerging only to poke gentle fun at our fellow travellers, and to tell each other stories about how those people lived when they went home, or what they might talk about behind closed doors.

My mother had a huge appetite for life, and a well formed and generous sense of fun. We sailed the Mediterranean to the sounds of her singing the "Hallelujah Chorus" at the top of her lungs, hiked through the mountains of Corsica to her rendition of the "Bohemian Rhapsody", and drove down through the East Coast of America to the sounds of her singing along to the "Best of Take That". Always she would sing and dance her way round the world while my father looked bemused but slightly embarrassed, my brother James would blush and my sister Ann and I would cry with laughter.

Where we would be afraid to do things, Mum would just march in regardless leaving us to run along behind, trying desperately to keep up in case we might be caught out by horrified passers-by. Whilst staying on an island where the accommodation was largely timeshare cottages, Mum would quite happily march in to any that appeared empty just to have a look around and see what was what, whilst Ann would stand outside feeling the need to keep a look out, and I would sneak in guiltily behind wondering if we would get caught, and wondering what we would say if we did.

My father, a much more reserved person, saw her every fault and yet loved her deeply and immensely in spite of all of those things, and also because of them.

The truth is she gave colour to an otherwise grey world.

Three: Margaret

My daughter believes we didn't get along when she was a child. The truth is I loved her deeply and immensely, but I did not allow her to get her own way. She was a sickly child; she suffered terribly from asthma and eczema and was allergic to everything. This often led to her feeling unwell, which tended to bring out the worst in her, as in the early days there was little in the way of medication which would relieve the symptoms, so she felt feeling drowsy and tired all the time, as well as extremely scratchy, in every sense of the word. Frequently when asked what she wanted Father Christmas to bring her for Christmas, her response would be "a new skin" and then I would have to explain that while Father Christmas could do many magical things, that was not one he would be able to manage. However, what her body lacked, her will more than made up for. She was a little fighter, and invariably she fought with me. That, coupled with my own stubbornness, led to a disharmonious household. Her door would slam; her music would be turned up a few notches. Her feet would stamp, and I would try to remain calm.

On one occasion, I tried sending her to her room as a punishment, but this led to the biggest and loudest tantrum of all, for she was not yet tall enough to reach her own door handle. She had her visiting grandfather in tears, pleading with me to "let the poor little maid out" before she became quieter, after a good twenty minutes of howling and shouting and stamping that would have awakened the Lord of Hades himself, and led to the family quietly referring to it as her "Rumplestiltskin" episode.

It was a battle of the wills that I believe neither one of us truly won. We simply learned to reach a truce.

And yet now I think I would give anything to see a glimpse of that fire in her, but all I see is water. She has no spirit left in her, my brave and strong daughter, and I fear that when she lost me, she lost herself also. Finding her way again will be a long and arduous task, and one that I hope she is up to the challenge of. For life must go on without me, and she and I will both need to find our own way independently in this labyrinth that we call existence. For "life" is characterised by change, and once change stops, you simply cease to exist.

Four: Charlotte

As I enter the hospital room, she lies quietly on the bed and does not stir at all. Her breathing is now peaceful, but her skin has a yellow tinge to it, which is deeply disturbing as it means that the cancer has reached her liver. Cancer is a small word for such an insidious, nasty disease. This particular one has taken hold of my once strong beloved Mother, and washed through her body like a flash flood, destroying everything in its wake in a matter of weeks. One month ago they told us that we would have at least six months together. Now they look grave and remain tight-lipped, while we draw our own conclusions. It will not be long now, and I know we are talking about a matter of days if we are lucky, or more likely hours.

Her once beautiful but now sunken face confirms to us it will not be long. Her hair is soft and brushed back against the pillow. Her skin is smooth and her face has not a single line on it. She is only sixty-one.

Somehow she always knew it would come to this. Her own mother left in this way, and was only a few years older than Mum is now, but I would give anything to have those extra few years now. Anything.

"I will never make old bones," she would always say to me with a wry smile. But then it was a vague and far off event. Recently though she was more obviously circumspect, even before the diagnosis came, she would never make a plan beyond the next few months. She knew long before the doctors did, but I think she shielded us from it. Always the protector, my beloved mother, always so quick to protect everyone else, but the last person she would look after was herself.

Time for us has not just run out, but it has stopped dead in its tracks. The world continues oblivious to our pain, just as we are oblivious to it. We are cocooned from it, encased in a shell which at any moment may crack and send us all sprawling on the ground to be trampled underfoot.

Outside in the world a terrible tsunami has swept away hundreds of thousands of people, hurricanes rage across America, and bombs drop on the Middle East, but inside this room we are impervious to all but our own worst private nightmares.

Mum sleeps on, her breathing peaceful at last, her face clear of the pain and distress she felt when she was awake and still with us. I stroke her hair while my father dozes in the chair on the other side of the bed.

Outside the day breaks on a cold January morning in Devon. The trees are bare and a cold wind blows off the high moors and into this wide valley. The window is open just a crack because she always wants to have just a little bit of fresh air. The heavy net curtain blows in the current. Somewhere a tractor starts up and I hear voices hushed in the corridor outside. Mum stirs:

"It is so peaceful here." She whispers, almost under her breath, and then drifts away again.

I lay my head on her pillow, place my mouth next to her ear and start to speak gently to her.

Five: Margaret

Death was very gentle when he came for me. He wore no cloak of black, he smelled not of decay, beyond the distinctive mulchy smell of the earth. He raised no bony finger towards me, his eyes did not glow red beneath his dark, empty looking hood. He came instead on a breath of fresh air through the window that was open just a fraction to the dark night air. He brought with him the scent of the dark hills beyond this valley, a scent of home.

My family eased my leaving for me, as they knew I had to go and that it was the best thing for me. This body was useless to me now, so sick was it, so frail, and so tiny in comparison to what lay beyond. My husband held my hand on one side lending me his warmth and strength, my daughter Ann sat at the foot of my bed, my son James leaned against the wall in the corner of the room, silent but watchful, overawed by what was happening, and my other daughter Charlotte, sat with her head on my pillow, an arm stretched around the top of my head while she stroked my hair and spoke soothingly of what lay waiting for me on the other side of the veil. She described in loving detail all the people who waited for me there; my beloved father and mother, aunts, uncles and friends who had gone before me, the cottage that would be waiting for me at the top of a high cliff overlooking the sea, where the birds would fly with joy in the cool sea breeze. The garden filled with jasmine and apple blossom, the old cat who would be sleeping by the fire, the old dog Henry, who we had loved so dearly, who would be sitting waiting for me at the door.

"It is ok to go, Mum," she said. "We know you have to go and it is ok. We all love you very much, and Granddad is waiting for you on the other side."

Bless them for their deep love in letting me go. They did not claw at me, as they may have wanted to. They did not desperately cling to me for dear life. Instead they loved me enough to let me go and be free.

Somehow I saw all of this although I still slept. I heard her words although my ears were deaf to them. I felt their closeness. I was wrapped in a blanket of their love. I can't say I floated above the room watching everything from afar as some may tell you; only that I felt as if I became part of each and every person in the room. The colours were somehow intensified, and I felt very little pain. There became numbness in my body, and somehow, something tugged me away from it, leaving only a lightness of feeling. Death took me in his arms and lifted me away from it all into a world of bright lush greens; thick verdant freshness that held the gurgling of a stream, the rush of wind through the trees, and the lapping of the waves on the shore. There was indeed the hint of jasmine and apple blossom on the breeze, and the warmth of the sun on my face and my back.

I felt like I had come home at last.

Six: Charlotte

Her breathing becomes shallow at the last, which we know is a sign that it is time for her to let go. The death rattle they call it, that sounds in a person's throat as their body begins the final shut down of all functions, the lungs start to fill with fluid and the breathing begins to stop. But still she remains calm as we soothe her with our voices and our hands. My brother James is silent throughout, not knowing what to say, and not wishing to interrupt us as we attempt to midwife her passing.

Her eyes suddenly open and become fixed on a point above us in the corner of the room. Her eyes do not waver for a second, and neither do they blink. She must see things we cannot know are there, and I pray silently they are good things. Her father reaching out a hand to steady her; her mother waiting to lead her onwards, glad to see her after so long an absence. Her long-since passed aunts and uncles ready to welcome her with a smile and a warm embrace. I can only trust that this is so.

A nurse comes in to check on her and immediately responds to my questioning look with a brief nod of her head. She quietly leaves again to give us the space and privacy that we need. I turn back to Mum and the sound in her throat becomes louder. A single tear falls from her left eye, and she exhales one last time. She is gone.

Death takes her in his warm embrace, and kisses the pain away. The pain for us is just blossoming, and now another journey must begin. Later, I pick up my pen and try to write letters to her, as it is the one thing that all the self-help books say you should do, write to your loved one as if they had just passed into the next room and not left your side completely. But I know I am desperately clinging to something of our relationship. If I do not, I fear I will drown in this. As a life-long journal keeper, writing it is the only thing I know how to do.

Part Two

Fear of the Dark

Seven

8th January 2005

Dear Mum,

It has been a week since you died, although it has felt like
a lifetime. I hardly think you would recognise us now; I
hardly recognise us myself. Life has become an alien
landscape; things look similar, but somehow not the same.
The grass is still green, and the sky is still blue, but they look
a different shade than they were before.

Yesterday I stood out in your garden, and the cold wind
blew around me leaving my fingers like ice. I took all of
those horrible cartons of Complan nourishing drink that you
so hated into the garden and stabbed them with a knife. I let
the watery milky liquid drain out of the cartons and into the
stream, to be washed away from us and sink back into the
earth. The water in the stream was so cold that my hands
began to ache, but still I continued with the furious stabbing
until I could no longer feel my fingers. Then I lit a charcoal
and burnt some incense in your honour. I sent it up with a
message of love for you, and as the rain began to fall, a vast
flock of white birds circled and whirled over the house. I
don't know if you received my message, but I wanted to lift
my head and howl into the wind like a she-wolf.

I miss the sound of your voice telling me to stop giving
myself such a hard time. I miss seeing you as you sat in the
chair reading a magazine, as you looked over the top of your
glasses at us. I miss your music, and although I have tried to
re-introduce it to the house in parts, it is sporadic, somehow
forced, and unmelodic. The songs that once caught at my
heart and carried my soul along with them seem somehow

uninspired and flat. Dull even. I miss your spontaneity, your humour, your wit and your laugh.

Life this week has lost its shine, its sparkle.

Your loving daughter
XX

Eight: Margaret

So strange this feeling of being without the physical body, so hard to imagine unless you can feel it and experience it, which of course you will eventually, one day. I am both light as a feather on a breeze, and heavy as a pebble thrown into a pond. I am everywhere at once, but that single word "everywhere" is not enough to describe the vast expanse of the experience. We see things as being defined by fixed borders when we are solidly attached to a body, but here the borders are blurred and shifting. They change and mutate like water, and yet are less fixed than liquid. There is no defined shape; there is no defined logic as you know it. Language, being a tool of logic, somehow diminishes its scope, restricting the shape to something tangible, when by its very nature it cannot be made tangible in that way. How can one use a tool of logic to give an image of something which apparently contains none?

I have become part of everything that exists, and more than that. At a molecular level you could say that what is me engages in the dance of life that is everything else. We are all one, and yet we are separated by concepts, by ideas, and by fixed and fixing language. I am at one with everything, and I can choose to be with everyone at any time, and in multiples. This allows me to sit with my husband as he looks into the flames of the fire feeling so very alone and vulnerable as he half listens to the Chopin concerto on the radio, and it allows me to watch over my darling little boy as he lies in bed trying to be grown up about things, fighting the unwelcome lump in his throat while he tries to turn away from his feelings, frightened by their magnitude. It allows me to be with my daughter Ann as she blankly stirs a pan of soup on the oven hob, which she will eat but not be able to taste, since her senses have all been dulled by the pain, and my daughter

35

Charlotte as she lies in a tepid bath, eyes and throat sore from sobbing, wishing desperately that Death would come and take her too, but knowing I would want her to live. She has now looked Death in the face, seen the yawning chasm, felt its seductive pull and yet has had to step back from it and attempt to go on as before, and yet she will never be the same again. Her life has now changed forever, and all she can do is move forward from here. All any of us can do is move forward from here. This I would tell her in a heartbeat if she could only hear me. I see her struggling and fighting the waves of grief, and then being overwhelmed by it as it washes through her nose and her mouth, drowning her in misery. If only she could look up and see me here, feel me or sense me in some way, she might at least know that I am alright, and that she will be alright.

It is as it must be for every man, woman and child on the planet, for every species. Life is immortal, for the living must die. Our bodies must die because they are merely mortal flesh, and yet our spirits must journey onwards. And so we continue in an everlasting spiral of birth, life and death, yet I know this will not comfort my beloved family now while they feel the agony of loss.

"If only we could have had one more day, one more year, one more decade," I hear their hearts cry out. Just one more anything would never have been enough, so they continue to mourn what might have been, and what will never be. The grandchildren they think that I will never know in the flesh, the holidays we will never take, the laughter we will not share knowingly. And yet I am still with them, with every fibre of my being, but they cannot hear me now, they cannot see me, and they cannot feel me. What cannot be experienced through the five senses is lost to them now.

And yet I am still here. I still exist. There is a world of experience beyond the physical five senses. If I could only write home and tell them I arrived safely, or give them three rings on the telephone like we used to in the past to signal that we were home, but too tired to talk, or make them hear me or understand my presence through the world around them. But they are deaf to my voice, blind to my presence. It is as it must be and I must accept that fact and be patient, and hope that one day they can reach out their awareness and just grasp for a second that I am still here, and that there is indeed something beyond the grave. Life does not stop dead at the point of death; it is just that we must leave our body behind and journey on without it. For in the world where I am now, a body would be a hindrance. They are so dense and so heavy that it would only hold me back, and now I must learn to live beyond the physical, beyond the eating, sleeping, breathing animal that I was before and move on into a world of light and spirit and freedom. For here while I may not enjoy some of the more sensuous pleasures of living in the flesh, I can instead enjoy the infinite nature of living in the spirit. It has a whole other set of pleasures and adventures just waiting to be experienced.

My only reason for grief is in the separation I must endure from my loved ones, until their time comes to join me here too. And yet even the apparent separation is just another illusion. I am still here, and I can still see them. They could still sense me too if they only knew how, but it is a skill that not many people are brave enough to develop. The holy books like to tell people it is wrong and evil and marks the path to evil, but that was because it kept people in line. Why have holy men if people realise they can do it all for themselves? It could put a whole industry out of business. If you teach people fear, they will learn to stop asking questions, and after a while they will even forget to have the thoughts that led to the questions in the first place. And a population that has forgotten how to think for itself is much easier to mould and control. But anyway, I digress. You didn't come here for a political or religious or moral discussion. You came here for a story, and I will distract you no more.

Nine: Charlotte

When we all left home my Mother turned my brother's old bedroom into a dressing room. It was not a large room, barely big enough for a single bed, but large enough for a set of cupboards down one wall and a dressing table which sits beneath the window. When I came home for visits we always had a ritual of Mum showing me all the clothes she had bought since my last visit, meanwhile telling my dad that it was just an old thing she had found in the cupboard that she had had for ages. Of course he knew the truth, but he would play along with the charade in order that she didn't feel too guilty about indulging in her love of clothes. Scarves, shoes, tops, skirts, trousers. She liked to look nice, and she always did. She had immaculate taste, my Mum, with an eye for the unusual, the fun. There were her "wizard coats", brightly designed and artistic looking patchwork displays of dazzling colour, and her dresses that she had bought for various functions she attended with her new set of friends, a lively and intelligent group of women who all enjoyed each others' company and experiencing new things in life, whilst keeping an eye on those less fortunate. There were lots of brightly coloured scarves, bought to dress up the classic black pieces she so loved, and shoes that would make Imelda Marcos sit up and pay attention.

I come here now to sit quietly and breathe in the scent of her. Somehow I hope that if I can still find a physical trace of her, that she is not really gone. I wait for the morning when I will wake up and realise it was all a bad dream, just a nightmare, but still it doesn't come. I wait for the night when she will come to me in my dreams and tell me she is alright and how I should now learn to move on and live without her, but that doesn't come either. The only time that I see her in my dreams, she is unwell and dying, a shadow of her former self not displaying her full warmth and richness of character and not the woman I remember who was so bursting with life. And so I wander aimlessly through my days and my nights, losing all hope of ambition or progress, but managing only to keep putting one foot in front of the other. I continue to exist, even if she can't, even if I don't want to. I must do this for her. I must keep moving forward in a Good Orderly Direction even if I am resentful of every single breath I take. Time takes an eternity to pass, and I mark its slow ticking with agonised awareness. One day. One week. One month. Then it is six months and a year. And still I secretly hope she will come home and tell us that we will never guess what a marvellous adventure it is that she has been having. Or better still that I will come home to where she is and not have to feel the pain anymore. I am continually amazed at how much pain a human can feel and yet still keep moving onwards.

I begin to wear her clothes. They are too big for me and they swamp me in their enfolding layers. They are too old for me, but somehow I can pretend in a corner of my mind that by pulling on her jumper, her scarf, her socks, I am sheathing myself in her warmth, in her love. But how quickly the smell of her on them fades and is replaced with my own, so I switch to secreting her things in a box when I am away from the house, so that I can open the box, take out her things and breathe her in when I am in my own home too.

And I can't help wondering; did she do this when her mother died? You see, in a strange twist of fate or something like it, her mother died at the same age, of the same form of cancer. And she was the same age that I am now. The difference was that she had children to look after as well, as my brother and sister were both very small. How would it be if I had a child to look after too? Did she stand in her mother's room as I do now, feeling like I am intruding, prying through her things. Did she breathe in the scent of her mother as I do now? And I wonder, what would she tell me if she was here now? How would she comfort me? What words of advice would she have for me?

39

The irony is not lost on me; that she is the only person I know who could understand how I feel, but she is not here to soothe me. The one person I would turn to in times of trouble is the one person I have lost. This world is a pale comparison to its former self, and it is cold and fraught with dangers I never even knew existed until now. My life has now changed forever, and even my body does not react to me in the same way it used to. The whole of my being now has an underlying sense of anxiety behind everything I do, like white noise in the background, or ringing in your ears, that is there inexplicably, but you don't quite know how or why. It will never leave me now, I will simply have to become acclimatised to it, but moments of warmth and human love will give me a brief refuge from the fear of life that holds me now. But conversely it is not a fear of losing my life that bothers me, I am not afraid to die. I am simply afraid to live, and afraid that living will carry on indefinitely. If someone could tell me now, "don't worry, you will only have X amount of years before you can go and join her" I might feel better about it all. Instead all that stretches out before me is life as far as the eye can see. The sky merges into the horizon, and there is no end in sight for me at all.

When you can't tell the difference between the sky and the horizon, it just becomes an unmanageable mass of grey. There are no waves or wind that I am aware of, no sunlight to highlight and pick out the varying shades of colour; it is just endless, flat and dull.

Ten: Margaret

What would I tell my daughter if I was with her now? Heartbreakingly, I am with her, but I know she is unaware of me, so cloaked is she in grief. Somehow, if I am ever to get through to her, she must lift herself out of this deep well of mourning. I am within the well of souls and here to be heard, if she will just listen out for my voice, but her ears are deaf to everything except what is within her.

If she could hear me what should I tell her? That her grief will pass? No, I will not lie to her. My grieving for my mother did not pass; the wound scabbed over and healed a little, but I was left with a deep scar. I never lost my grief, but I did learn to live with it as one gets used to a physical scar. I learned to control it in public. Gone were the days when I would walk round with tears pouring down my face, almost oblivious, instead I learned to hold the tears for a private moment. I got used to living with it.

That is what I would tell my girls, that they will become accustomed to living with it as one gets accustomed to a physical imperfection. It becomes part of what makes you the person that you are, and after a time it cannot be detached from you. The bumps and scratches and imperfections become a living breathing story of where you have come from and what you have endured and learned. We are so much more than just the sum of our parts.

My own Mother, Violet, steps in close to me.

Eleven: Violet

My daughter is perfectly truthful in what she says. We are more than the sum of our parts, so much more. But as well as the environmental, personal experiences we also take so much from those who have gone before us. I see in my granddaughter, Charlotte, much of what was in me, although she won't remember anything about me. I left that world two years before she was born, so the only memories she has of me are the stories told in the family, and yet we are so alike in life. My husband, her grandfather, called her his little Violet after I had gone, because she was so clearly made of the same stuff as me. The temper she showed so much as a child? That was mine, and my Mother's before me. The asthma and allergies that made her so ill and helped her be seen as difficult? They were mine too. People thought I was difficult too; a difficult old cow some might say. I would challenge them to a life of illness without medication, and then see how they judge me.

The dead live on in the memories of the living, and once those who remember you have gone, all that is left is your genetic stock which lives on in your children, your grandchildren, and your great-grandchildren. Fame is fleeting and localised; it is no way to leave your mark on the world. Genes live on forever, forever changing and mutating, yes, but there nonetheless. If you could open a window into what lies beyond the world, to see what you had borrowed from your ancestral family, you would be surprised at the familiarity you would see there. Charlotte has never been able to understand why her feet just can't bear to be covered up when she is in bed; no matter how hard she tries to keep them undercover, she will always wake up with all of her, except for her bare feet, tucked warmly under the quilt. Her feet will be ice cold and free, moving constantly. She always thought it was just her own idiosyncrasy, until she tucked her mother into the hospital bed one evening, and just after the nurses left the room Margaret said to her, "Untuck the sheet at the end will you? I can't bear having my feet covered up." Charlotte smiled at the revelation and did as requested, filing this information away to comfort herself on the long dark lonely nights.

We all carry elements of our ancestors in the most surprising of ways, not just in the colour of our eyes, or the shape of our noses, or the shape of our bodies, but in much more subtle ways, like the way you walk, or the way you squint into the sunshine, or the way you chew your food. The ages of humanity and its history, entire generations, all pass in the blink of an eye. Life is short; my granddaughter will join me and her mother soon enough, but for now she has work to do.

Twelve

Monday 10th January 2005

Dear Mumsie,

Tomorrow is the day of your funeral.

This morning we went shopping in Ashburton, and as we passed by the funeral director's building, I had a brief awareness that you were in there, but it was not really you who was there. I saw you in each and every shop I went into. I comfort spent, I will admit, as if somehow I thought it might bring you back closer to me. Although I never got to go there with you when you were still here, I could spot each place, each item that you would have liked. But I found that after two candles, one packet of joss sticks, one body cream, two soaps (and £35) later, you were still not there.

We delivered the flowers to the abbey restaurant in preparation for your wake, and then came home, dejected, to have a late lunch with the others.

It is funny now that I remember you saying in November,

"Next time you are both down, you and Ann can go shopping in Ashburton."

At the time I was angry that you had such a defeatist attitude. That was about ten days after you told me that you had cancer, and that it was inoperable. That was about forty-eight days ago. How swiftly it took you. And I suspect now that you knew long before you told any of us, but I don't resent the fact that you needed time for yourself to work things out. I know you always considered us before you considered yourself, and it was about time you took something for yourself.

I keep thinking, "This time two weeks ago, we still had you and we were doing this…" but somehow it doesn't help; time still glides by regardless, and the day of your death keeps repeating itself in my memory. And regardless of how I play it out in my mind's eye, I will always lose you.

After lunch, it was time to be on the move again, time to visit you in the Chapel of Rest. As we parked the car and got out, something in me thought, "Phew! Now at last I will get to see Mum, after all this time!" I felt a buzz of anticipation, even though I knew you would not be in there. And you weren't. The thing they showed me was not you. It had your hair, and your nails, your beautiful hands. But it was taut, perspiring cold from its forehead and just so small. Empty, fixed and just not you. If I was unsure before, I came out certain. I would not find you there.

We came home to plants on the doorstep from your special friend Marianne. I went with Dad to the pub to meet her and her husband. And Aunty Jane and Uncle Lawrence had also just arrived from Boston. Marianne cried when she saw me, she said I look just like you. We talked for ages, and she is lovely. She told me of her shoe fetish, and her problems when it comes to packing. I was too polite to tell her you had already mentioned those things to me. But she did tell me how diplomatic you were when you tried to suggest she might like to think about just how many pairs of shoes she needed to pack for a week in the Scillies. As I left, she hugged me and said you had told her she would love me. I was quite shocked. I still feel as if I could always have done more for you. I worry if I did it right, when I talked to you and stroked your hair as you were dying. Did I say all the right things?

On Wednesday we will walk with Marianne to your grave, but for now I must sleep.

XX

Thirteen: Charlotte

I stumble across tufts of heather and gorse, my feet becoming entangled in their woody stems, breaking into a stumbling run. But running to where? I seek solace on the open Moor, but all I find here is echoing emptiness. I may lie on the earth and be soothed by the sound of the river that tumbles over granite and through peat, but the earth that cradles me is cold, hard and wet. Not the warm enfolding embrace I so badly need.

When I look back on this time a year or more from now, I will barely be able to mark out distinctive days or events. It will be a forgettable blur of sadness. People will later recount conversations they had with me, and I will have no memory of them. I am insane with grief.

"Look up."

I shake my head. Am I hearing things?

"Look up, lovey."

No. That wasn't my imagination. Mum? I lift my eyes and catch my breath. I stand on the brow of the hill and the earth spreads out in front of me, joining with the sky at the horizon. A sky that has turned orange, and golden, streaked with dark cloud and bright light. Night comes down over the Moor like a shutter pulled down by the rugged beauty of the setting sun.

"There is still life to be lived," she tells me, and I resent it. I resent this assertion. I would be happier if she would take it back and instead tell me when I will be joining her. But still the golden sky holds my attention, it mesmerises me and will not allow me to look away. I hear the sound of the wind blowing through the trees in the forest on the other side of the valley, and it sounds like the waves lapping against the shore. What solace I can find in nature is laid out before me now. Dewar waits in the forest below astride his horse, its front hoof beating the ground, impatient to ride, his hounds hidden

by the dark shadows between the trees; Pan dances as he plays his pipes in the valley by the small waterfall in the Wallabrook; Hecate holds aloft her lamp and the intersection of three paths worn through the heather by roaming sheep and ponies, reining in her dogs, but my Mother is conspicuous by her absence, except in the faintest breath of the breeze. I could almost sense her words finding their way into my consciousness, like the faintest of fragrances carried on the air.

And still I know this is nature's way. Life is immortal, for the living must die. Every single creature on the planet must sooner or later experience the death of its mother, and it must be far worse for a mother to lose her child, knowing that it is not the natural order of things. I must endure this as every other creature must, and I know I can find her if I try hard enough, but somehow I don't know how. *I don't know how.* She must still be here somewhere. But all I hear now is the wind singing in the couch grass; and all I feel is the cold bite of winter on my face, making my nose run and my eyes water. The dark descends around me, blurring the outlines of the tors against the black night sky. The cold starts to seep through to my bones before I can bring myself to return to the home that is empty of her warm physical presence, but shouts her name and resonates with her passing in every room. She is nowhere in that house and yet she is everywhere. Just an echo of her remains; she who was so full of life has left here now.

I make my way over to the bookcases that line one wall of the living room from floor to ceiling. In among the books, one shelf is given over to boxes and boxes of family photos, some in albums, but most still in the paper envelopes they arrived in from the developers.

"We must have a good sort out," she had frequently said to me over the last few years. Another way in which time ran out for us.

"Ran away screaming," she corrects me in my head. I can't quite bring myself to look at the photos now. I fear if I do, I will lose all semblance of sanity, as tenuous as it is. Instead, I take from the shelf an old hard-backed book, "Baby's First Book" it says on the front cover above an old fashioned picture of a brown teddy bear holding a bunch of blue flowers that look like forget-me-nots, but are too large. The paper inside is now browning with age, the writing done carefully in ink is now fading. It is my grandmother's curled and neat writing, recording faithfully the milestones of her beloved baby daughter's first few years of life. She cut her first tooth on November 30th 1945; she had her first bathe at Cawsand beach on July 7th 1946; Christening has been neatly crossed out and replaced with "her dedication" which happened at Hope Baptist church in the presence of Mrs Esme Sheridon and her Aunty Rose. Her first words were "Mama" and "Dada" and "No" which has been underlined twice. How like my beautiful mother to know her own mind so vehemently at such an early age.

I start to sleep with a photograph of my grandmother on my bedside table, hoping she will watch over me just as carefully as she watched over my mother. I can't yet bring myself to look at photos of Mum as I know if I do I will fall apart. Grandma is just one step removed, but safe enough to be my angel of watchfulness while I sleep; I am newly afraid of the dark, since Mum died, and I feel like I need all the help I can get. I look like Violet, people tell me. Her mirror image they say. The fierce sense of pride in me also hopes that I take after my mother, and that I will be worthy of her memory.

Fourteen: Margaret

Funerals really seem to bring out the worst in people. Two hundred and fifty people have turned out for mine, and I feel quite honoured. They pack out the little village church, drenched by the horizontal rain that falls outside, and the wind makes the heavy oak doors of the church shake and the slates rattle. The candles flicker at the front of the church just at the right points in the service, the doors clatter loudly just as the Vicar speaks of me as being gone but never forgotten. I couldn't have planned it better if I had tried. It was as if I stood at the back of the church giving stage directions through the cans:

"And cue thunder and lightning," just as the church becomes momentarily lit by the light show outside. I imagine God shaking the sheet of tin outside to give the sound of thunder, and then the show must begin.

My special friend Ruth is sitting four rows back in the centre. She will meet my daughter Charlotte for the first time today, although she has met the rest of the family before. Strange to think they have never met before, when both hold such a central role in the last four years of my life. Ruth will be a beacon for Charlotte through the many dark nights of the soul that are to come. I tap Charlotte on the shoulder and direct her attention to Ruth. Unaware of why she must look round but unconsciously knowing she should, Charlotte looks round and for a moment they experience recognition, although they were never formally shown the way to each other. Ruth dabs her eyes beneath her enormous black hat, and they smile at one another. Although they have never been formally introduced, their connection to me shimmers in the half-light of the candle lit church.

But there has to be an equal measure of bad for the good. Although life does not exist in black and white, still there must be balance. There is the person who knew our family fifteen years ago who will come up to Charlotte and with all sincerity say to her:

"It must be so much harder for your sister Ann, since she got on with your Mum much better than you did."

Charlotte will stand with her mouth slightly ajar for a few moments, before collecting up her dignity with a smile and moving on. Then there are the people, who will sob on the shoulders of my family and say:

"I just don't know how I will cope without your mother. She was my rock."

To these people again we will hand a tissue and move on.

When you attend the funeral of a dear one you must leave your pain and grief at the door and attend to the needs of the others. There is no place for private grief here. They are not all bad, and they do not mean to be bad, but somehow they are not "firing on all cylinders" as my father would say. They are the same people who sent me cards for my last birthday that said "Many Happy Returns" even though they knew I was dying. Were they asking me to haunt them? Perhaps I might rattle their windows tonight, just for fun.

But for now I will linger around those that loved me best, and try to lend them my strength. For this is one of the most difficult of days. I have rallied the troops on this side of the divide to bolster those left behind and we are all working hard to help them through it.

It is a heavy burden they carry for me, and I am immensely proud of them for doing so with such dignity. They speak their truth quietly, but clearly.

Fifteen

Wednesday 12th January 2005

Dear Mumsie,

Yesterday we had your funeral, and I learned about the LWDO.

The day dawned cold, dark and blustery. The rain was not only falling down in droves, it was falling sideways. The wind was whipping it up and under our brollies, and wrapping it around our legs. The men who carried your coffin stood by your graveside with no umbrellas, and the water was pouring down their faces and dripping off their noses and collars. I wanted to offer them a tissue or an umbrella, but I know they are expected to just stand there and endure it without complaint.

We all stood and wept as they lowered your lovely willow casket into the earth, not knowing the difference between Nature's tears and our own. Then we came back to the house for prayers and to dry off. The whole family stood in a circle to pray, which appealed to my pagan sensibilities. We were all there; the full extended clan, including Uncle Lawrence and Aunty Jane from Boston.

From there, we all got into the funeral car to drive to the church. The service was good and very atmospheric, nature put on a very good performance to contribute to your send off. We had gales howling round the church, rattling the doors and the tiles on the roof, and a trumpet player to accompany the hymns.

As I sat in the front pew, I snuck a look behind and spotted your "special friend" Ruth, dabbing her eyes beneath a wonderful black velvet hat. I smiled at her when I caught her eye, a strange way to meet for the first time, I know, but somehow I know we will like each other.

We put a copy of your favourite photograph of you (the one you said was the only one you ever liked – you on the London eye with your hair spiked and leather jacket in hand) blown up large and framed. It looked beautiful, and I thought it may help people to remember you as your healthy self. James placed a lit candle beside it, which danced and flickered in the draft, and we all read for you. I held my breath as each of us stepped up into the lectern, but each of us managed to get through our piece without cracking or wailing. You would have been proud of us, Mumsie, but we wanted it to be done right for you.

I spotted someone halfway through my reading that I did not want to speak to, so I am afraid I shot off as fast as I could after the service. I just couldn't face talking to them on that day of all days. I made the excuse of showing Uncle Lawrence and Aunty Jane how to get to Buckfast Abbey, but in my haste I forgot I had the keys to Dad's car in my handbag. Dad and James ended up having to hitch a lift to the wake with the Vicar, who was most accommodating and took it all in his stride.

The refreshments do at the Abbey turned out to be as well attended as expected. We estimated about two hundred people plus, as not everyone came from the church to the abbey. I think it says a lot about your life, Mumsie, as Ann said in her reading, "How well did you live? How well did you love? How well did you learn to let go?"

There were plenty of wailers, some weirdoes, and also the nice people (who were the majority). The family split up and "worked the room", as it were. Every time I tried to eat something, I would be tapped on the shoulder by someone fresh wanting a conversation. Jeremy Wakefield's mother showed me a picture of her grandchildren (surprisingly pretty); Jean Grant tried to talk about work; Victoria Eastman managed to spend the whole time talking about herself; and Rick Hampton managed to tell me that he expected Ann would experience your loss more than me as she had a much better relationship with you. Yes, I know he is an idiot who knows nothing, and we haven't seen him for fifteen years so what would he know about how well we did or didn't get on, but nevertheless it did leave me gaping as if he had just slapped me with a wet trout!

Once we shook off the stragglers, the especially close people came back to the house for a big pot of Dad's chilli and chats. To be honest, this was the one part of the day when we could relax a bit. Your special friends are indeed very special. Ruth tells me that I should expect to hear from you soon. She also tells me you told her tales of Ann and I sloping off with Andy down the lane when we were younger, telling you we were just drinking Earl Grey tea when we were in fact smoking marijuana (tee hee!) And what is this I hear about you booking "LWDO" meetings in your diaries as a way of sloping off for shopping trips? Apparently I do not qualify for a "Luscious Women's Day Out" as I only have a B cup bra and I would need at least a D cup!

I am glad to hear that you had such nice times with your friends. I was beginning to think your whole time was spent in social-working the lame ducks. It is a relief to know you got to have many a laugh and a giggle. Oh, and Ann and I decided to adopt Ruth and Marianne as our Fairy God-Mothers. What do you think?

All my love,
XX

Sixteen

Monday 17th January 2005

Dear Mother,

Two weeks and counting. While you were ill time seemed
to move so slowly. Such an awful time, and yet now I look
back on it I savour every minute of it. But now life has
resumed its former gallop.

I am back home, and due to start my first day back at
work. I feel scratchy, tempestuous, little miss fire cracker,
almost willing people to say something clumsy and ill-timed
so that I can unleash it a little, and whip them sharply about
the face with my words. Of course I know that would be
unfair, so I will it to nestle down inside my belly, coiling
around on itself, hissing its forked tongue as it dozes in a
light sleep.

How the landscape of our lives has changed with your
passing. Ripples spreading out across the pool, and a handful
of pebbles dropped in. Ripples upon ripples upon ripples;
stretching out to the outer edges of the pool.

Later:

The end of my first day, and it all feels a little
disconnected, not quite like real life. I connected to life in a
different way when you were ill. Every decision we made had
more resonance. Every conversation felt like it had more
meaning. Our pain was magnified, but so was our joy. When
I told you that "I love you" I know I meant it from the pit of
my stomach, from the very core of my soul, from the centre
of my beating heart. Now you are lost to me, I cannot seem to
feel it, to even feel anything else anymore. It all feels surface

level, plastic, man-made fibres, something that will fall apart the first time you wash it.

Sleep well my lovely, n'night.

XX

Seventeen

Tuesday 18th January 2005

Dear Mum,

The world marches on, oblivious to your passing, and I
want to scream at them,
"Don't you know? Don't you know we've lost an angel?"
Instead I walk on, eyes turned down to the ground,
connecting with nobody, crying inside.

XX

Eighteen

Thursday 20th January

Customer Relations
Human Mortality Department
Nature Unlimited

Dear Sir / Madam,

    I feel compelled to write to you to complain vociferously in the case of my Mother, Margaret Payton (28/12/43 – 1/1/05)
    It is my sincere belief that a terrible mistake has been made, and that you have recalled her too early. As you can see by the dates above, she had in fact only just turned 61 years old when you claimed her. Surely this is no age at all, when the so-called "Holy" book cites three score years and ten, and advances in modern medicine have led people to expect eighty or even ninety years as being the norm.
    My mother was, in my opinion, in her prime, and still had many tasks left to complete down here. I understand that my complaint will be received too late to have any actual effect on the outcome of this matter, but I wish to have my dissatisfaction formally recorded at how your department handled this situation. I do hope not to encounter the same lack of foresight and planning in future.

Yours faithfully,

Charlotte M. Payton (Ms.)

Nineteen: Violet

Margaret must step back for a while and let others take over the role as guide. She has her own journey to complete, and if she remains close to those on the other side of the veil, it may impede her own progress for all souls must progress and move forwards, no matter which side of the veil they exist on. Margaret must spend some time in the healing halls so that she can prepare to move into her new role. I don't mean healed physically; since the physical has no place here, but she must be given time to reflect and report back on what she has learned, as well as to start to come to terms with her own transition. She can't do this effectively if she is thinking about other people and what they are going through. For once it is time for her to be a little more selfish and leave the guilt behind her.

The rest of us now must step forward to take a more active role in supporting the ones left behind, and both sets of grandparents will play a part now. This is the role of the ancestors; in time we must all assist those of us who are left behind. They must petition us for help, and we must step forward and do whatever must be done.

I am well used to this work now, although since time is not linear, I cannot say for how long I have been doing this. It is the space of two physical generations, and yet it has taken me a brief moment to get here. A level of experience and time does not ease the difficulties of seeing your own family members in distress, even if like some of us, you did not know them well in life, you knew them well on this side of the veil before you or they went into the physical life. They are still connected to you by the golden thread of kinship. They carry your genetic coding, which you took from your own ancestors. We must step up to the plate as it were.

If they could only see what we see, and remember what they knew before birth they might find this part easier, but then that would diminish the lessons they could learn in life, so we are limited in what information we can pass on or remember in the physical world. The whole point of a physical life is to feel things, and if there was no uncertainty in death, what would be the point? If I told you that you would live forever, would you still make sure that you got out of bed each morning and gave each day your full energy and attention in order to keep moving forward and learning new things? I expect you would not, because you could always wait until the next day, or the day after that. Sometimes it is already hard enough trying to do the things your heart yearns for, as we think there will be time next month, next year. That is how we can spend our whole physical lives, never quite managing to do the things we always wish we could do. There is always a wish, and an "if only" so imagine how it would be if you had forever.

Most people would put it all off if they knew this was not the main or only event. That is why they tell you there is no dress rehearsal in life, because if you thought this was not all real, you would not do the things you came here deciding you wanted to do. You live in a holographic universe. This does not diminish the sense of loss you will feel when you lose a dear one, but it will also not diminish the joys. You must experience pain in order to know what true joy is; they are two sides of the same coin. Janus who guards all gateways has two faces, and so does life. Too much of this certainty of something beyond could lead to disorder and misuse of the knowledge – look at the Victorians. They believed this life was nothing in comparison to what would come later, and what did they have? Great chasms in society between the rich and the poor, because they all "knew their place" and held out for a better time in heaven. Life could happen in the most appalling circumstances, and no one would ever take steps to improve another person's lot in life, because all that really mattered was that when they got to heaven they thought it would all be different. The sad but simple truth? "Heaven" is what you make it just as life is, but it should not be held out for at the expense of living a full life and grasping every opportunity with both hands.

Life may happen in shades of grey, but it is easier to navigate if you can think in black and white. Life may not be characterised by good and evil, but feeling love and pain are common to every life. And so, if you chose a mortal physical existence, you must choose and embrace the pain as well as the love.

The soul's capacity to experience these emotions never ceases to amaze me. The depth and the sheer force of will required to keep going under such conditions is immense. And yet without them, existence would be grey and flat and the lessons would diminish. A life lived in a half-lit twilight world of no feelings is a life not fully realised. And that is the point.

Only I can't tell Charlotte this now, for it would be the last thing she would want to hear. Hindsight is a luxury only enjoyed after the event when we can look back. Now is not the time for retrospection, for that would be to inflict a punishment on my darling girl for the life's lessons she must learn for herself.

I remember when I was a young girl at school, my Headmaster used to call us all into assembly each morning, where we would sing hymns and then have a parable read to us which would inevitably contain some lesson we should hear and consider and learn from in earnest. Ironically many of those tales still stay with me now, so he fulfilled his intention. He once read us a story of a little boy who stood and watched in awe as a butterfly emerged from its cocoon, amazed at how much it struggled and fought its way out over a period of several hours. When it emerged, the butterfly displayed a dazzling array of colours on its wings, and the boy watched as it flew out into the garden and out into the sunlight. Later on he came across another cocoon, and remembering the deep and heart rending struggle of the earlier butterfly, he took out his pocket pen knife, and carefully cut a slit in the cocoon, thus enabling the butterfly to emerge with relative ease. It emerged quickly, and stopped for a moment to unfurl its delicate wings before flying away, but as it did so, the boy realised with a sinking heart that the butterfly had no brightly coloured wings, they were grey and flat-looking and dull.

A life without struggle is a life without lessons. And a life without lessons is flat and colourless, and has no contrast. One day Charlotte will look back on this and be able to identify the brass among the dirt, but for now, I will not be the one to try and point out the obvious to her, for to her it is not obvious. It is her life, her will and her lesson, not mine. All I can do is be there to watch her unfurl her wings, and try and see that she does not get eaten up by the nearest swooping bat, like the moths that used to fly to her bedroom window at night, or be damaged by the storms that lash around her, and hope that one day she will thank us for gifting her with this freedom to learn for herself. One day we will all sit around the fire and trade stories of our times in the physical world, but for now she still has stories to gather.

Twenty

Sunday 23rd January 2005

Dear Mumsie,

Twenty three days ago we had just lost you. What a Happy fucking New Year that was, as I am sure any one of your clients would have told you. You used to laugh about them coming into Probation and saying to you,
"Sorry, Margaret, but it does my fucking head in."
Somehow that seems strangely apt now. I can really share their sentiment.

The constant lump in my throat has developed into tonsillitis, and although I have been to the doctor and got some antibiotics, I am not sure they are doing anything. I am feeling distinctly sorry for myself. Three days of bed rest already, too many soluble aspirins for my liking. No wonder you hated all that medication we had to give you. I have one painkiller to take every four hours, and I feel like I would rattle if you shook me. For the whole of your last month and a half you had so many pills. A month and a half? The whole of your illness in fact, pitifully short, painfully short, no time at all. For that I am thankful. Already I am getting glimpses of you more clearly as your healthy self than as the sick self we had to wash and walk across the bedroom to the toilet. I felt your bones through your skin so quickly, so quickly. How quickly the body can waste away and be reduced to a shadow of its former self.

Today I am missing you so much. I miss you every day, but some days it is more bearable than others. Tonight as I write, the tears are rolling down to drip off my chin onto my chest. They are quite cold as they run down my cheeks, and make me shiver inside.

I missed talking to you this evening. I spoke to Dad, James and Ann, but I have avoided everyone else. I want to hibernate, to crawl under the quilt and hide from the world. I want to come with you today. I have had this thought before, that I wish I could come with you already. I don't want to be here anymore. It feels as if the colour has bled out from the earth, the sound has been turned down. I can taste little, I wish to touch nothing and have nothing touch me. There is no fun, no sparkle here. I am she who loves life no more.

I can't feel my purpose here anymore. But please don't think I would do anything drastic; I know you would never condone that. I know you were two years younger than me when you lost your Mum, and you had two children to take care of, so what do I know?

When I think about how much of your life you lived without your mother, I realise how little I know. How little I know of love and life and struggle. When I see what you achieved in your life, I see that I am barely a tiny piece of the person you were, I am not as good a person, I am not as wise, how can I live up to you? You were so special, we were so lucky to have you, I can't see how we could either live up to you or even fractionally compare, let alone improve on what you were and what you did. I know this is not a competition, or rather I think I do. But losing you has made all the things I used to worry about seem pretty mundane. So that makes me question, what is the point of life? Is it to progress? Is it merely to tread water? Is it to love? For what better teacher could I have had?

I wish for many things in life, some material – I wish I had a house with a garden, and a big kitchen to brew in. Some of my wishes are for my soul to be able to sing – I wish fervently that I could earn a living creatively – any of the ways in which my soul really expresses itself. Now I work with computers, and while that might present a scientific challenge, but they don't really do it for me in that way. They do not float my boat, they do not inspire me, and yet I am still grateful to have found a way of being useful in life. I like working for the charity, I just wish I could find ways to be more creative.

My most fervent wish of all, the most all-possessing, all-encompassing wish of all; that tears out my insides and leaves my heart faintly expiring on the floor, is that I wish you had not been taken so soon.

You were my friend, my beloved, keeper of my heart, my love, my conscience, my guiding light, my dearest Mumsie. I will miss you for as long as they keep me here.

XX

Twenty One

Dear Mum,

I am sitting in your favourite chair at the house writing this letter to you. Today was my first trip out for many days. I got up early and caught the tube to Paddington (bleurgh! Via King's Cross in rush hour!) Then I caught the train home to Devon. Of course I did not travel "peasant class" as Ann calls is, so the journey was comfortable and remarkably quick. No sooner had I picked up my book than the man announced that we were about to arrive in Exeter St David's.

Dad and I have done his shopping, picked up some nice daffodils for you, and then after lunch we walked up to the graveyard to put the flowers on your grave. The wind carried a bitter bite from the North, so we did not linger other than to tidy the flowers that were there and put them in water. Even the cards on your wreath have blown away now, all except those from Ann and I. Again, I was struck by the simple truth – you are not there either. I keep wishing I could find you, as it just doesn't feel right. Your shoes are still in the garage, along with your coats; your dressing room still smells blessedly of you. I can almost feel you sitting beside me now, but I can't bloody see you or hear you. It is most infuriating. I can't even seem to catch a glimpse of you as you turn a corner ahead of me; I was at least expecting that, to at least feel a ghost of you haunting me, just a little bit.

Despite the cold, there is a faintest whisper of spring in the air. A single primrose amongst the stones on the track, snowdrops bow their heads in the hedge and crocuses spring up from the lawn. The final apple has just fallen from the tree and already the spring comes to challenge winter. She taps her watch sharply, her long flowing dress shimmering in the late winter sun.

"Almost time you were going," she reminds Winter; now bent and old beneath his velvet cloak of ice.

I remember that you always loved spring, and always loved spring flowers, so I feel sad that you did not get to see one more with us.

Yesterday I had a really bad bout of the mean reds. I flopped around the flat all feeling lethargic and miserable and no use to anyone. While I was cooking dinner something came unleashed and I started to cry. The tears were literally pouring down my face and I was howling so much and so loudly, it reminded me of the sound that the cowardly lion from the Wizard of Oz made, but all I could think was "Where do all these tears come from? Aren't I going to run out soon?" but somehow they didn't, and they just kept falling and falling and wouldn't stop. It is almost as if I can step outside of myself and laugh at the ridiculous spectacle I make, and yet I am powerless to stop it because I just feel so awful.

I seem to switch alternately between two moods at the moment. The "fingers-in-ears-la-la-la-I-cant-hear-you" mood, where life seems like normal, and the "doubled-over-in-pain-and-howling" mood. Obviously the former is more comfortable, but I am aware it is not real; it is merely an illusion, whilst the latter is far more real to me somehow. Anyway, what feels strange about this letter writing is that I feel a bit self-absorbed and impolite and I want to ask how you are, and what things look like where you are. Do you think they might permit you to write one short letter? No, I suppose not really.

Missing you with an ache,

Your loving daughter,
XX

Twenty Two: Margaret

It is a strange experience to stand at your own graveside and watch your family tend it lovingly. They chat to me as they clip and arrange the flowers, carrying a bottle of water with them all the way up from the house. They tell me about what has been happening while I have been gone, and of course I am there with them as much as I can be, but I also have to move on and take up my new role here. In order to do that I have to recover, but while it seems so much easier for me to heal than it is for them, I still have my own grief. I miss them too. So occasionally when I can, I check in and see how they are. In time I will be stronger, and may be able to stay with them for longer periods, but for now I, as well as they, must look forward not back and not get too attached to the grief. We must process it, learn to live with it, find other ways of living and move on.

I too mourn the loss of what we will never have. I think a lot about the things I had planned to do, and although I will still get to do all of them in spirit, there is something most special about experiencing them in the flesh. For life is not all pain and discomfort. Otherwise, why would we choose to live in the physical life if it was all bad? Life is also full of wonder and magical experiences if you know where and how to look for them. We choose where we come, and we decide our own fate. We come into life for a reason, to try things out that we have been curious about, to learn valuable lessons and to keep growing in ways that we can only begin to grasp at in the physical world.

But there is a special pain in hearing your loved ones speak to you and not being able to answer back. Well, I can answer back, but they do not know how to hear me, which makes it a bit futile really. Were it not for the ones that guide me in my transition, it could be frightening. Just like Jimmie

Stewart in "It's A Wonderful Life", a person could run round the places of their former life in a blind panic, desperately trying to make someone hear you, someone... *anyone*, while the world marches on unblinking, unfeeling, unhearing. But I am learning to be at peace with my apparent silence. There is a serenity in silence I have only newly learned to appreciate.

I must trust that things will work out well, for they will. These are not completely new frontiers we are approaching. After all lots of people have lived and died before us for generations, for millennia, and in truth we are not disconnected from the rest of humanity, even though we like to think we are. We are all linked by the golden thread-like bonds of love, even though we are mostly unable to see them. Everybody in the world is loved by someone; even Adolph Hitler had his Eva Braun. None of us are alone, even though sometimes life can feel like one of the most solitary, lonely experiences there is, and when we are alone we feel that we must be the only person on earth to feel this way, to have ever felt this way and the only person on earth whom nobody cares about. In life I learned that someone must always step forward to give love to the unloved, caring to the uncared for. Divinity is found in love. It was my role in life, and I know it was no accident. Now I am on the other side, my role will be much the same. I will guide those who are lost; I will give comfort to those who are in pain. But for now I must trust that my dear ones will be better served by someone else, and that for now I need to step back and trust others to play this part.

Twenty Three

Monday 31st January 2005

Dear Mumsie,

Well, I had a good but difficult weekend with Father. On the Friday night we went to the village pantomime, which was dedicated to you. It was good fun, but longer than I expected! But I have to say the biggest shock was James Mudge playing the dame – I couldn't get my head around that painfully shy and quiet farmer, who could hardly say boo to his own goose, transformed into a blonde curly corset-wearing, Queen's English speaking dame! We were greeted like royalty that evening, and bumped into Judy and Hilary, who were quite shocked at my affirmative answer, when they asked if I had ever done the pantomime. It made me feel quite nostalgic. I went straight home and leafed through the old photo albums from the 80's, when I was "child number 3" on the cast list. Ironic to think I had more regular acting work in those days than I did when I moved to London and got my Equity Card.

The cast invited us back for the after show party on Saturday. I have to say I single-handedly made several of them cry by walking in with a home baked Homity Pie. Dad asked me to make one, in honour of you. Jill told me that she got all weepy on the way over, thinking that what would be missing was "Margaret's Homity Pie." I made it just as you would have made it, with your old recipe.

I am sorry to say that on Saturday during the day we took your car into Exeter and sold it. It felt awfully harsh to do it, but I have to say that what Dad got for it will cover your funeral expenses, so I am sure you would be alright with that.

Anyway, I know you always got frustrated with its stupid little engine and the way people treated you differently than when you drove the golf. So Betsy is gone, and there is a large gap in the garage where she used to be parked.

Luckily, we still have your dressing room. It has been so comforting to go in there, and just smell the scent of you all wrapped around me like a blanket. I do feel like I am intruding rather, and I hope you don't mind, or think of me as somewhat of a magpie, but James, Ann and I agreed we could each have a piece of your jewellery, as a way of keeping you nearer. James has a gold ring of yours set with a star-shaped sapphire, Ann has your locket, and she has added a picture of you in it opposite the one of me. I have your talisman ring, but when I put it on my finger, I felt like a girl dressing up and wearing her mother's high heeled shoes. It is yours, not mine, and I would rather you were here to be wearing it instead of me. When I wear it my hand reminds me of your hand, my fingers are reminiscent of yours, except that my nails are not as beautifully looked after as yours. I also took your silver pill box as it is just the right size for the lock of your hair I kept, and I will place it on my bedside table, to keep you near me while I sleep.

Dad has been putting together an album of pictures of you, and it is lovely. I noticed two beautiful truths in it: firstly, that we have so many pictures of you we are very lucky, and secondly, how in all of them you are smiling, broad and wide. You had such a beautiful smile, and it is nice to hope that you had more to smile about in your life than to frown about.

I do worry terribly about Dad, but we are all doing our best to try and see that he is alright. I hope we are helping a little, as he is devastated to be without you, as we all are.

Love,
XX

Twenty Four

Thursday 3rd February 2005

Dear Mumsie,

Month two, and I think it is only beginning to hit us now. Ann and James both ran away to Spain for a few days with their friends (separately that is.) Sadly, they both came home saying that you would have loved it.

I am thinking of doing an MA in creative writing. I can't afford either the money or the time, but an MA is something I have always wanted to do. I seem to be bingeing on filling my mind with as much new information as I can find at the moment. The Microsoft course continues in a couple of weeks, the tarot course is going well; my official "spiritual" studies have taken a back seat for a while, but will kick off again on Saturday. But I have noticed something different in myself now. When I was a younger person (I know 31 is not over the hill, but I mean when I was 18 or so) I seemed to want to study so I could be "clever". Clever in the sense of feeling more clever than those around me, as a way of feeling special or different. These days I am questioning myself a lot to ensure that is definitely not my motive now. I can't remember you ever elevating yourself in that way. I don't remember you ever putting someone else down to make yourself feel good about yourself, and I wonder; were you always like that? Or was it something that you fought long and hard to become? Of course, if you were here I may ask you, but just as easily, I may have been too embarrassed to ask. It is a very personal question after all, and I know when you were alive, your modesty would make you blush and giggle in the face of such hero worship.

71

Missing you Mumsie.

Love,
XX

Twenty Five: Violet

Often grief brings with it an overwhelming desire to fill the immense hole that has been created by death. But just how do you fill a hole that big? It would be like throwing a pebble in the ocean.

I stand beside Charlotte as she starts trying to fill the minutes, the hours with any old stuff she can find. If she keeps her mind busy, maybe she won't have to think too hard about what is happening. But really it is all just a momentary distraction, and sooner or later she just has to sit down quietly and allow the tide to sweep in. For when the Nile floods, fertility returns to the land.

I see the flashes of disbelief on her face, when she stops for a moment, I see her howl in desperation, when she relives the last few months. I see her wander round in a daze made of insanity, leaving her belongings wherever she goes, a bag here, and purse there, half listening to conversations around her, hurting inside and stuck firmly in a bubble of her own grief. It will take time to erase the pictures in her head of Margaret cut down by that disease, of Margaret on her death bed, of Margaret's empty shell left behind after she had gone. Those images shock to the core, and are immensely private. You will find no grisly details here. They can never be shared with anyone, not a single soul. When Margaret knew she was dying soon, she asked for no visitors outside of her husband and children, and her special friend Ruth. She said she couldn't cope with other people seeing her looking so ill. Some people took offence at this and were angry at the family for shutting them out, but they did it to protect her. She did not want a great queue of people lining up outside the bedroom seeking forgiveness or a blessing before she left. She wanted some peace and privacy. These images of Margaret as a sick and dying woman, they can't be discussed even within the family. Each person will keep them locked securely within themselves to protect her dignity, and to protect anyone they could tell, from the horror they have seen and still see when they close their eyes at night and try to sleep.

In time they will begin to seek out images of her when she was well, but for now even that would be too much. Instead, Charlotte keeps a photograph near her bed of Margaret aged eight years old, her blond hair cut into a neat bob, with a large bow of ribbon sweeping her fringe to one side. She smiles the wicked grin she always smiled, but her features being so much younger, enable Charlotte to distance the image in her mind's eye, from the image of her mother close to death.

I remember the day that photo was taken. Margaret came home from school excited by the visit of the photographer, and she had painstakingly made sure that her uniform was kept immaculate, and that her hair was brushed until it shined. That photo was promptly copied and framed, and placed on the mantelpiece of every one of her aunts and uncles. She was the apple of my eye.

Margaret was a late baby, as I had not expected to have children at all. I was told early on that it was not possible, and I recall the delight we felt when she arrived. In those days forty was frowned upon as an age to have your first child, so I was treated somewhat as a side show by our community and by the doctors, who prodded and poked and rubbed their chins thoughtfully and discussed me as if I was not there. But when she arrived, Margaret was the bonniest, happiest baby you ever did see, and she won the heart of everyone who peeped into her pram and saw her beautiful blue eyes and her delightful smile.

Not that she was a *good* girl all the time, she had a wicked glint in her eye that she got from her Aunt Rose, and she was forever finding mischief, but she was bright as a button. The fact that her first words were not only "Mama" and "Dada", but also "No" gave her Father and I the clear message that

74

she was a force to be reckoned with. She was the kindest most loving girl you ever would meet, but god help you if you tried to pull the wool over her eyes!

I was very ill by the time she reached nine years old as I suffered from severe asthma, and in those days people didn't know how to treat it. There were no medicines like there are now, the only thing a doctor would prescribe was sea air, but living on the coast meant I had plenty of that already. You just had to live with it and hope that it did not take you by force. We had to send Margaret to live with an aunt for about a year, and I missed her sorely, while she was away. That year was the saddest year I ever knew. By the time I was well enough to have her home, her aunt was so taken with her she asked if she could adopt Margaret. That would have broken my heart and her Father's, so of course we refused.

The reason for me telling you all this is that it pains me to see Charlotte's agony, because I know how it feels to have Margaret taken away like that. I know *just* how it feels. And yet the world keeps on turning, life goes on and you must claw back a semblance of a life, and filling every minute of your waking (and sometimes sleeping) existence is all you can do to keep yourself and your sanity on the same train together. You must do whatever it takes to pull you through this time. But ultimately all the money and drugs and alcohol in the world cannot take this pain away.

Charlotte must learn to walk again, seemingly all on her own, although she will have help from the other side there too. But to all intents and purposes, she must believe she has learned to walk again all by herself. For every child must learn to become an adult; and that involves independence and will power. She is not experiencing anything that others have not experienced before her. But still that does not make it any easier, when it happens to you. Life is about overcoming challenges, but it is also about experiencing joy.

Twenty Six: Charlotte

My world has turned grey and cold around me. It is as if someone has pulled out the plug to let out the water, but all that has spun and whirled down the plug hole is the colour, leaving everything in an outline of grey on grey. It feels like a film noir, but without the promise of redemption at the end.

It is cold here, ice cold. And I seem to have entered a world of intense solitude. Generally most people I know have avoided me. It is strange, but when I enter a room I see people avert their eyes and I feel their discomfort. They are so desperate not to make eye contact with me and they are hoping I will not speak to them, because if I do, they will have to say something, and the truth is they don't know what to say. What can they possibly say? What words could make a dent in this situation? I feel like the walking dead, a leper; people see me and they are thankful they are not me, but they don't want to get too close in case I rupture like a water balloon in front of them and leave a steaming, stinking puddle on the floor.

But the strangest experience by far is my friends' reactions. People I met only in recent years have rallied to try and bolster me, they sit and just listen and allow me to say what I feel, or even better, they are willing to sit with me in blessed silence. There are not many who can handle the silence and you must be brave to allow the space for it. It is deafening, deadening, crushing and crushed. And yet they allow me this time just to sit and support me through the pain.

People I have known longer however have not been seen for dust. The ones I thought would be with me until the very end, the ones I thought would be with me through anything, side by side and through thick and thin, have vanished in a puff of smoke, and only emerge through brief text messages once in a while, when their conscience reminds them to check

76

on me. Somehow I had expected they would come to the funeral or at least offer to, but they did not, and I was quite shocked. I needed to feel them with me, and yet they are gone. Not only have I lost my mother, but I have lost my former life as well. Saturn has made his return with all the force of a nuclear explosion and it has all crumbled and fallen around me like the lightning struck tower.

And yet I can no longer fear death coming for me too, as he is constantly at my side. It is he who has become my gentle companion in the dark nights, whenever I draw the tarot cards he is there at the centre of everything, waving at me with his bony hand and his toothy grin. Standing knee-high in the bones of those he has cut down, I feel his presence in all that I do; I see his face all around me on the faces of people in the street, on the cold empty branches, in the slate grey skies. I have developed the ability to know how we will all look when we have died; I look at every face and see its own death mask features frozen in eternal sleep. It is a skill with a limited application, and I speak of it to no-one. It would not be my first choice of a special gift. I would prefer the ability to fly or see the future, not death.

He is almost tender in his consistent presence, I almost feel his warm embrace, and I feel safe in his care, a safety that the outside world just can't give me. For there is now a constant level of anxiety in the pit of my stomach that I never knew existed before. It hisses like white noise in the background, or like the constant irritation of tinnitus, but it never diminishes or goes away. I have started to get an inkling of what I have lost. With the presence of my Mother came a level of security and reassurance that I will never know again in this lifetime. Acknowledging the loss of that security breeds an underlying fear that permeates everything I do, hence my sudden fear of the darkness. And yet it is not really death that frightens me, it is life. The thought of living makes me feel anxious and sick, and yet it is something I know I have to do.

But overwhelmingly, I know that if I am to survive this and make a new life, which I must for her sake at least, I must pull myself out of this pit of despair.

Twenty Seven: Margaret

I step out of my front door and into a world of colour. The light here throws a distinctive pinky hue on everything, but somehow the colours are sharper and deeper, and the tones are vivid and bright. I have never seen such brightness in physical life, but here it all seems perfectly natural. The air is warm where I am, not too hot, but this place seems to have a nice temperate climate. And yet the plants and animals that are here are extraordinary in their variety and abundance and are almost tropical looking.

My garden is large, and dotted around with beautiful mountain ash trees and fruit trees. So far I have identified apricots, figs, apples and almonds. But what is unusual is the fact that the trees are simultaneously weighed down with vast amounts of blossom *and* fruit, something I never saw in life. A large jasmine climbs a trellis at the front of the cottage, and in the evening when I open my front windows to let the air in, it sweeps delicately through with the scent of the jasmine and the apple blossom. All of the cats I ever adopted and loved seem to lounge among the herbs and the agapanthus that bloom soft blue in the flower beds, while my special house cat sits contentedly in front of the fire with the dog we all loved so well in life. They keep me company in the times when I am alone, but mostly I have lots of company. My mother and I sit by the fire in the evenings, while my father tells us of whom he has seen and met with that day. It seems that here you can meet and talk with anyone you would want to meet and talk with. They both update me daily on how our loved ones are progressing, for move forward they must, so they are spurred on gently by those of us on this side. Soon I will go back and see for myself, but for now I must acclimatise to this new existence and decide how I am to progress. I must see and learn and dream of what I will do next. For here the only limit is the limit of your imagination.

By day I step outside of my front garden and walk to the edge of the cliff top, where steps are cut into the rock leading into a wide secluded bay beneath. The sand is white and glitters in the sunlight like pure crystal. The water is turquoise, clear and shining and full of fish that swim and dart in all directions, flashes of jewel-like colours that glide and move in the water. I sit on the soft sand and watch flying fish as they dart through the warm sea and leap through the air, their scales flashing blue and silver in the bright light of day. Out in the bay seals bob their heads above water and invite me to come in and play. And when I step into the water, I feel its warmth seeping through me and healing me to my very core. The salt soothes my aching spirit, and my former fear of deep water has vanished. Here I can swim as well and as freely as the dolphins that leap from the water ahead of me.

When finally when I step out of the water, and make my way back up the cliff-side steps, I see an abundance of sea plants growing on the side of the cliff, reminding me of the places I loved so well in life and the warm days we spent walking the coastal footpath in Cornwall. But here the colours are more intense, the profusion and diversity of life is more abundant, and it is all here for the enjoyment of any who chose to be here.

An eagle circles overhead, not in search of prey but simply for the pure joy of the freedom and safety of the winds. Back in the garden small birds chirp to welcome my return, but while I see wrens and robins and blackbirds like at my former home, I also see hummingbirds hover to sip the nectar of the myriad bright flowers that grow here.

I exist in a world of colour and light.

Twenty Eight

8th February 2005

Dear Mother,

This morning I received a whole six-page letter from Zoe from school. I was so pleased; it gave me a real lift. With all the emphasis on instant communication these days, I had forgotten the real pleasure of receiving a hand-written, slaved-over letter. I felt like Elizabeth Bennet!

The sun is shining and it is one of those beautiful crisp winter days, with just a hint of spring in the air. Yesterday morning I walked through Regent's Park and saw thirteen herons, all standing around the lake. As I walked on further and looked up, one flew overhead with sticks in its beak. I traced it over to the trees in the distance, and there sat its mate, next to a half-built nest.

Zoe's mum has just re-married; you will be pleased to know. It is lovely to hear that she is happy, after having such a difficult time before. And Zoe is still working in Glasgow. I will have to write back and tell her what a wonderful holiday we had, when we stayed at Loch Lomond. I will always treasure it as a golden time with you. You seemed so well and happy and bursting with energy. Thank goodness we didn't know about the tumour then, as it must have been there, lurking in the background, ready to strike in barely two month's time. Looking back it is difficult not to see the early signs of the illness in your face, but I do not want to spoil the memories of our last happy holiday.

One thing I am struggling with is my resentment. I feel like fingers scraped down a cheese grater the wrong way. I feel rawness, hotness, and it darts out of me at times and in ways I can't seem to anticipate. I will give you an example. Someone on the television this morning spoke about nearing their fiftieth wedding anniversary – you and Dad only had forty and I feel angry about that. Whenever I hear people talk about their mother as being a certain age, I think in terms of what you (and you and I together) never had. I see old people in the street and feel resentful that you will never get to be that old.

It is not their fault. It is not anyone's fault, but it is unfair. And that thought is very quickly followed by the certainty that everyone in life will experience this. There is no escaping this. Death and taxes springs to mind; the old adage about the only two things you can count on in life being death and taxes.

So then I start wondering what the point of life is. So, Mumsie, I have become a walking cliché! And I always thought I had been put here with a purpose that was different from everyone else. I always thought I was special, arrogant little girl that I was, and you just accepted me. If only I had known then that no one is different from anyone else, if only we all knew this fact, the world might be a much nicer place. And yet you were the one who gave me unconditional love, my life's blessing. I will always be thankful that I had you in my life as such an important figure. What more can I say?

Love,
XX

Twenty Nine

12th February 2005

Dear Mum,

It is strange but it is only recently that I have realised that I am not unique. I was walking home from the tube having been for a haircut in Upper Street, and it suddenly struck me that every single person I could see, and ever would see, will at some point (if they have not already) lose their mother. It is natural. It is the way of life, of nature, that it will come to an end at some point.

People have told me this, and I have nodded at their sage wisdom. I have even thought it before. But it is the first time that I have really felt that thought; truly felt it. I will not say that it lessened my grief at all. That would be a lie. But it shifted somehow. As if something that I had worn as a cloak before, something that blanketed me from head to foot, had shifted slightly.

I was able to feel the grief in a palpable way, in my heart, my throat, my solar plexus, blocking off all other parts of me. I can physically feel two distinct knots beneath and behind my shoulder blades.

I began to feel that not only have I lost a wonderful angel of a mother, but I have also lost my friend, my mentor, my conscience. You were the voice in my head, and my heart, my bench mark, my yard stick. The one person I was always pleased to spend my time with. And I wonder if any part of you is still in consciousness, in "life" in some form? Out in the world, open to the elements.

All my love,
XX

Thirty: Margaret

Dearest Charlotte,

The beauty of this existence is that not only am I out in the world and open to the elements, I *am* the elements. I can turn my attention to a gliding flock of birds and become them, not just one of them, but also *all* of them. Their collective consciousness is open to me. The whole of existence is open before me and ready for me to be part of every little detail of it, or its whole entirety.

I have flown around the world in a way I was never able to in life. I always regretted the fact that I had not travelled as widely as I would have liked, and yet now I can see my heart's desire and travel to the very centre of the universe. I can dance in the wide heavens amongst the stars, paddle my feet at the shores of the warm Indian ocean, swim to its depths and see the wonders from deep inside our own beautiful planet.

I have stood under great waterfalls feeling the water pound against me and yet flow through me and with me. I have felt every drop of water in its excitement to rush towards the sea. I have felt air molecules brush lightly against me and been caught up in their whirlwind joy of whipping dry leaves up against the grey winter sky. I have danced amongst the flames and felt the warmth of the sun. I have felt the cold damp earth and been part of its intricate layers, and tunnelled to witness its deepest darkest secrets.

My life force knows no restrictions. I am part of it all, and at one with it all.

I have visited the Alhambra palace at dawn before the crowds encroach on its deep peace and solitude. I have stood at the top of the spire of St Paul's, right on top of the dome and felt the freedom of infinite possibilities, and I have floated on air currents over the deep wounding gash of the Grand Canyon.

This landscape is testament to its history, and yet it is so fleeting, so fleeting. Each of us struggling through life cannot see how we all intersect and become part of a seething powerful whole, whose energy pulses like a heartbeat and yet will rise and fall like waves on the shore.

As individuals we are so tiny, so fragile. As a whole mass we forget what we can achieve, and so each of us is closed to the possibilities of what might be, as we get so involved in the day to day details and forget to look above it all.

I am here to be experienced, my love, if you can just cast your eyes heavenward and see me glinting through the dark clouds as a shaft of sunlight, floating on the breeze with the leaves, or blowing as the wind through your hair. I fall like rain on your face and yet you must learn to seek for me again. There is a universe of possibilities out there, if you can just lift yourself out of the darkness. Come find me on the open moors and let us dance beneath the moonlight and lift our eyes to the stars.

I am waiting for you there.

Thirty One

Wednesday February 16th 2005

Dear Mum,

It is strange, but somehow I still can't quite believe you
are gone. It doesn't seem right, or true.

When I spoke to Ann last night, she asked me if I would
like to go back to Scilly in April, if I don't mind sharing a
room with her. When she asked my initial thought was a
resounding no, I can't do it, not so soon after November
when I was there with you and you had just started to show
signs of your illness.

How can I go there and see all the places I have had such
poignant and happy times with you? The bench over looking
Old Grimsby quay where we used to sit and compare notes
on life and love; the bench overlooking the bulb fields
beyond Borough Farm where we would sit and turn our faces
towards the warm sunshine; the Foredeck, our favourite
clothes shop, for which we would leap off the boat and
scuttle along the main road in Hugh Town.

And now I begin to wonder if all those things were your
favourites too, or if I am already showing signs of putting
memories on you that didn't exist for you, just like all the
other lame ducks. C.S. Lewis talks of how he was afraid of
turning his wife into a doll-like version of herself in his
memory, having her perform for him what he wanted her to
say and do. Am I already doing that to you, Mumsie?

When I awoke this morning, your voice in my head was
telling me that Ann and I need to start to make our own new
memories without you. All of us have to. But it feels such a

heartless thing to have to do. And I anticipate it feeling so very empty without you. Empty and pointless.

XX

Thirty Two: Violet

Strange how we always assume that the truth is a rigid thing that always remains fixed. So much of society is built around "the truth" that is fixed and never changing, like a granite dolman that stands tall against an ever changing sky. The "truth" is that even granite changes over time. Its face is weathered by the driving rain, the howling wind and the warm summer sun. We are all constantly in a state of flux, and the only thing that never changes is that one thing: that the world, and we in it, are ever changing.

One person's view of a single event will always be very different from that of another person who witnessed the exact same event. Each will filter it, delete things, and distort others, until their internal representation of that event gets filed neatly away in the gestalt to which that event relates in their mind's eye. And since each person's filters are unique, each internal representation will be unique. These lines will mean something different to you than to the person sitting next to you, regardless of whether that person is your mother, your child, your sister, your lover, and they will mean something different to you than to me as the person forming the words. The world is a place that is teaming with life; each unique individual consciousness has its own unique world view.

So Charlotte's memory of an event may differ wildly from her Mother's own unique view of that same event, and yet both are equally valid, just as the meaning of a story is different to the listener and the story teller, and yet they are both engaging with the same story. We each take from an event the truths that we need to take, and yet fixing its meaning would be like trying to nail jelly to a wall. It would slither and slide away from you and form its own shapes where it chooses to land.

New memories will come in time, through no one individual's choice. Events will change, new adventures will occur. There will be new life, new laughter, new loves and new tears, whether Charlotte chooses to engage with them or not. You cannot fight the tide and turn it back, however heart-broken you may be.

The simple truth is Margaret had to do this when it was time for me to leave her behind. I left her when she was twenty nine, which gave her thirty more years or so of new memories and new experiences. To deny this would be to deny your own existence, your own purpose. And life cannot be denied when it is nature's will that it exists. Just as it cannot be denied when it is nature's will to take it away.

Thirty Three

18th February 2005

Dear Mum,

I have no words for you today. I simply want to be. With myself and with you, and with the Great Cosmic Joker.

Your loving daughter,
XX

Thirty Four

21st February 2005

Dear Mumsie,

Well, I went to see my friend the Psychic last week, just like we discussed last month. I say "discussed" because I am pretty certain that was what was happening, the morning I awoke mid-conversation with you.

She told me that you are alright, that you knew you were going before you were diagnosed, and that we probably will have found things organised for us. That would explain why we found the article about willow caskets in your desk drawer, and all the "How to Deal with Losing Someone to Cancer" books I found so neatly arranged on the bookshelf, all still in their pristine state, unread and waiting for us.

The fact that she mentioned your hair pretty well freaked me out.

"What is it with your Mum's hair?" she asked me, as I fiddled with my amber locket in which I have a lock of your hair.

She also told me that it wasn't a bad passing for you, that you had done all you were here to do. An angel, she said, just like I suspected.

So tell me Mum, were you reading over my shoulder?

Missing you with a vengeance,

XX

Thirty Five: Margaret

My sweet, I do read over your shoulder, I do see through your eyes, and I do know what you feel. For your eyes are my eyes, and your feelings belonged to me once. I sit with you now as you travel though the cold days here, trying to make sense of it. Do you feel that slight feeling of warmth seeping into you and somehow making you feel safe again? That is me by your side. Do you feel that pause for breath in between your sobs? That is me also.

I stand at your left shoulder, and try to infuse you with my love. And yet whilst you flounder and struggle to draw breath, it is harder for me to reach you. You and I both still have so much to learn about our new lives; for you must learn to rise up above the despair, and I must learn how to lend you strength without diminishing my own. And I must attend to my own development, if that will help to give you the determination you need to keep moving forward. Every soul must learn to keep moving forwards.

I can read over your shoulder and yet I can also hear the thoughts in your head before you can will your fingers to record them on the page. For your thoughts are my thoughts. I am your Mother, and yet I am also you, and the child you will yet have. Your breath is my breath. Your will is my will.

We are closer than you can possibly ever imagine. The frameworks of physical consciousness are too limited to enable you to see the reality of how we fit together. We are merely a breath away from each other, a single golden thread away, and yet you must lift yourself up to see me.

I will wait here until the end of time if necessary, to greet you when you too come through the transition. I will lift the veil for you, and beckon you to come closer, and then we will all be together again in the cottage by the sea.

Thirty Six

22nd February 2005

Dear Ma,

In my tarot class this week we had to spend time with the three "bad boy cards", Death, the Tower and the Devil. Everyone in the class was groaning when our teacher gave out the homework. I did not. I mentioned to him that my "current situation" in one of my readings last week showed death side by side with the tower. I have a feeling the devil was in there too. We both laughed at the irony, but it was nice to talk to him about it, as he is one of the ones who has been there before me, so to speak.

So he knows. There is no comparison drawn, like "When I lost my Gran," or "when I lost my dog" (which someone helpfully tried to talk to me about). I know grief is grief, but as my teacher said when you lose a parent, you literally come face to face with death itself. No veils, no intermediaries, just you and it.

I suddenly realised this week that my death card conspiracy does not only refer to your death Mumsie, but also my own. By losing you I have lost myself completely. The hard bit now is in trying to identify myself, amidst this stream of consciousness (and this scream of consciousness) and trying to put myself back together, to identify the pure me without you. And yet it is like making a cake and then trying to take the eggs out afterwards; once it is cooked, it is cooked, and there is no going back to what it was before.

Unfortunately, you were my most solid point of reference, my stencil, my mould. It's like pouring plaster of Paris into a bowl and expecting it to take shape of its own accord, but somehow I have to do it and be the one who moulds it.

Hopefully you are still there to guide me in essence, my beloved Mother.

XX

Thirty Seven

3rd March 2005

Dear Mumsie,

I have spent the last week and a half battling with the
plaster of Paris, so I am sorry I have not written.
Many worries crease my brow. I feel so old suddenly,
jaded and creased. My flabby bits have dawned on me. Life
has jumped up and bitten me on the ass; the stick insect is
long gone, the child all grown up now. I wonder what you
would make of me?!

I went with Dad to the formal dinner organised by your
friends at the Soroptomists in Plymouth last Saturday. I know
you know that already, for you were there in spirit. At one
point I even felt you standing off to one side watching us. I
did not see you; I merely saw the space where you were.
Maybe it was just my imagination, but somehow I don't think
so. It was the same sense I had of Aunty Rose standing at the
front of her funeral service.

Anyway, I suspect you helped me choose an outfit as well.
I am not used to formal events! But what I wore went
perfectly with my pink shoes, so thank you for that. And I got
your message from Ruth, when she came back from the
ladies' room she asked me what piggies were. "Check for
piggies," you told her as she stood and applied her lipstick at
the mirror. Well, I have never heard anyone else referring to
bogeys as "piggies" so it makes a good code, particularly as
we would always stop and do a "piggy check" before leaving
the ladies powder room, particularly when we were
somewhere smart. But Mother, couldn't you have told me

something profound like how to get published, or... where the lost family fortune may be buried?!

I love the fact that you have your sense of humour, and I like the idea of you having some mischievous fun!

I miss your warmth. It is cold here now.

Love,
XX

Thirty Eight: Margaret

When I think back to the time when I lost my own Mother, a thick fog descends and blankets my memories, so that I can't quite recall the day to day details of what happened and when. It is almost like amnesia, grief, and yet it is somehow ignored by our society. They make great films about those who suffer from amnesia, the undercover spy trying to find their own identity, being chased around America or Europe by those not wanting them to remember who they are. But grief is somehow hidden. It is wallpapered over, as if we don't have to engage with it, it won't really happen to us. I suppose that there is an outside chance we will never be knocked on the head and wake up to find we are a knife-wielding martial arts expert, but death will always caress your face at some point. And when he does you will be at your most naked, your most vulnerable self. There is no mask you can put on in his presence, no suit of armour that will protect you from his touch.

When I lost my Mother, I lost the ability to think clearly, just at the point when you need to be able to think clearly. There is the funeral to arrange; you must choose a funeral director, choose a coffin, choose burial or cremation, choose what your lost and loved one should wear, whether they are to wear make-up or not, open casket or closed. Then there is the service, what hymns to choose, what readings to have, where to have it and what to feed everyone, where to be buried or scattered. Then later, what words should be chiselled into stone for all eternity to express the love you felt for this person, and still feel for the rest of your own life.

So I prepared for this, on behalf of my loved ones, so that when it was time for me to leave, just a few of the choices would be made for them. Somehow I always knew it would be cancer that got me; the odds were not stacked in my favour. I chose the willow casket and left the details in the desk drawer where I knew they would find it. And I arranged the cancer books on the book shelf, all new and unread, ready for them to find. So few self-help books are useful at this time, and it is important to choose carefully. I wanted to avoid the stark, cold, heartless books that will tell my family I chose this end and somehow, unconsciously, brought the cancer on myself, although some fool will foist a copy of that particular gem on Ann. Choose this end? Who are they kidding? I was just beginning to enjoy myself! Why would I choose this painful, uncomfortable, nauseating end? And yet we all have to go sometime, and what takes you through the veil is almost immaterial when you accept that it is just your time to go.

But the constructive books are also there. The kind, knowing ones, for them to take or leave as they see fit; they may read and forget, or dismiss, or they may provide a much needed light through so much darkness.

When the darkness descended on me I too lost control. There is a quality in grief that can only be described as madness. I felt like I was living in Breugel's worst rendering of the fiery pits of hell. Had I been able to, I would have gladly shaved my hair off and coated myself in thick clay, to have it dry and crack and chafe my skin, to show the outside world a clue to what was going on inside. But somehow, unlike other cultures, our society seems to have lost the ability to witness and mark grief, so that people can understand it and recognise it for what it is. It is one way in which the Victorians got it right. At least it was clear how deep the sense of Victoria's mourning was when she lost her Albert; the fact that she dressed from head to toe in black until she herself joined him made it perfectly clear. The first madness of grief may pass, but the sense of loss I felt for my parents never left me. It became my ever loyal companion for the next thirty-odd years, and while life went on and I experienced a whole other lifetime, ask me about my Mother thirty years on and the Well of Souls would open before me and the old wound remained open. The serpent grief would rise out of the depths, strike me down and swallow me whole yet again.

But love can still cross the divide. It is just a case of learning how to recognise its ebb and flow, its rise and fall with the tides, its slow burning embers, its calm solidity beneath your feet, and its cool caress on your face. The sad irony is that to know I am here, they must raise themselves up to feel me, and yet grief will drag them down to the depths of despair, far away from where they can feel my presence.

Time will pass for them there, but it will be the blinking of an eye here. They must learn again to experience the joys of the physical world, before their time comes to join me here. That way, and only that way, they may sense my presence.

I never told my children, but when the madness of grief took me, I was so oblivious to the world around me that I got arrested. One day I wandered out of a shop still carrying the wire shopping basket without realising. It was only when the security guard stopped me that I realised what had happened, and by then it was too late. They treated me very harshly, and were not interested that I had just lost both parents in the space of two years. I don't want that to happen to my girls. The stain of something like that stays with you and people do not choose to understand. Maybe that was why I inevitably ended up working with people, who had committed crimes. I always believed people do the best they can do with the resources they have available, people are not their behaviour, and maybe, if that security guard had given me a break and listened to my explanation and not been so quick to judge and punish me, things would have been different.

If you can only give people a chance to shine, they will usually do so and not let you down. People used to look at me strangely in the street because I would stop and chat to the strect drinkers who sat in the bus station with their plastic bottles of homemade hooch, a noxious mixture of surgical spirit and cider, but I knew they had to be there for a reason. Life had thrown them for a loop. Had it been any different, had they been treated differently, they might not have been there. There but for the grace of God go all of us. But most people don't like that view, they like us all to be neatly segregated into our little boxes. They don't want to acknowledge that underneath it all, we are all made of the same substance, the same basic elements as the stars, all of us. We are all special, not just the ones society chooses to honour with fame. But it is not until you can face your own imperfections, your own divinity, and that of every single person around you that we can begin to make some real progress here. Leave your ego at the door and stop thinking about what is in it for you, and you start to see the world through different eyes.

We all wear the faces of the gods. They are many, and they are diverse. And they are beautiful.

Thirty Nine

Monday 14th March 2005

Dear Mother,

I worry that I am forgetting. I seem to spend so much time spreading a veneer across my inner self, creating this illusion that everything is ok, while inside I am dying, and a nuclear winter is blowing through my soul. I feel like I am losing touch with myself, and I am also losing touch with you.

And I have so much anger, it frightens me. It rises up from the pit of my stomach like lava. I can't believe the world is still turning, life is going on, the clocks did not stop ticking for you. How dare they? Don't they know who you are? See, I am even too afraid to use the past tense to describe you, for if I do, I will... I will what? I will die? No, I asked for that and that wish was not granted. I will cry? Yes, that goes without saying. I cry a little every day for you. Sometimes I cry a lot. Great sweeping gusts of weeping; messy and wet. Where does all this water come from? And yet I am getting bigger, not shrinking. I am getting a sticky-out belly at last, and a fat ass. I am no longer a stick insect.

I miss you, and I wish I knew how you were getting on.

XX

Forty: Margaret

Dear Charlotte,

You will never guess who I have been spending time with lately – your daughter Emily. Of course you do not know she is your daughter yet as you have not even thought about having a child, but my granddaughter Emily is here with me and we have been having a wonderful time getting to know each other again.

Emily is a lively spirit, and she is very much looking forward to coming to spend some time with you all. The main thing she wants to explore when she comes is being creative, like you. She says to tell you she is looking forward to having you teach her how to paint, as she has been watching you work and she thinks it looks like great fun. I have also suggested that she ask you to tell her about your "brewing" as you put it. Herbs and essential oils seem so soothing, and it will be a nice skill for her to learn from her mother.

Emily has been taking me to see a lot of the museums and galleries. We go there just after dawn before anyone else is there, and the wonders we have seen would make your hair curl in anticipation. So far we have been to the Cairo museum and seen the wonders of Tutankhamen's treasures, the Natural History Museum in Washington, the Louvre in Paris, but by far and away our favourite so far has been the British Museum. The Great Court has been our favourite place, to stand beneath the great glass ceiling and gaze in wonder, and from there we have looked at the statues from around the world, and nosed amongst the treasures in the back rooms when no one is around. It is just fascinating seeing behind the scenes. We have watched a lady painstakingly restore a bronze statue of a young man which has been tarnished green and battered by the years, but despite this condition he still looks very handsome, and we have seen how years of dust and grime have been cleaned from an oil painting of a little girl who stands eyes wide at the sight of what is in front of her. We have sat next to families as they sit and eat at the cafe in the Great Court, and Emily has promised to take me somewhere else soon, to a great vast library. It looks just like the Reading Room and the Great Court, but there are no books there as such. I will look forward to that outing and tell you more about it as soon as we have been there.

For now I am enjoying getting to know my granddaughter and revelling in her company, for I know that before long she will need to come and join you there.

Sending you all my love,

Mum
XX

Forty One

Tuesday 22nd March 2005

Dear Mumsie,

Yesterday was the first day of spring, officially. The equinox fell over the weekend, and we all gathered in London for James' birthday, even Dad, despite the fact that he always professed to hate it here in the city, and he seems to have enjoyed himself.

We had dinner at the Ivy to celebrate, lunch and après dinner drinks at James' friend's bar, and then we walked around the Tate Modern and spent Sunday sprawling in James' living room reading the papers. And not a single minute went by when we didn't all miss you. I think you would have found the Ivy interesting. Whenever we go to places like that with James, I always think of them as an adventure, or as a holiday where we get to see how the other half live. I know you would have thought it was all a hoot, and would have looked forward to telling Ruth all about it.

I have booked myself in for some counselling, because I fear if I don't get help, I will collapse in a heap. More and more these days I feel my surface beginning to crackle like ice on a puddle as you step on it. All the liquid oozes out of me, until I think "Surely I will dry up soon?" But I don't dry up and the tears continue to flow and they will not stop. I need plugging, a finger in the dyke to prevent the cracks from spreading any further. I know I will have to let it go eventually, but unless I do it gradually, it will overwhelm me and everyone around me.

I long to ask you how you are and if you have seen Granddad or Henry or Aunty Rose, but I hear only silence.

I must go now. I am sitting in the middle of a busy tube and I can feel the tears coming. The wailing is imminent!

Much love,
XX

Forty Two: Margaret

I remember a day in March several years ago when I visited the South Bank with Charlotte. It was one of those beautiful spring days that surprise you with its unexpected warmth. The sunlight glittered on the Thames and warmed the concrete, leaving us to walk around in thin tops and without the winter wrappings we had worn for the last few months.

I had come to London with my new set of friends to visit the House of Lords, and we had spent a lovely few days in each others' company; shopping, having dinner and doing a bit of the cultural stuff too.

Charlotte took a day off work to come and spend my last day with me, before I went home, and it really felt special, almost a turning point for us. She met me at the Bed and Breakfast we had been staying in, and yes, I could have stayed with Charlotte but I always liked my independence too much to impose on my family and to be frank, it was too much fun to miss the opportunity of staying in the same place as my friends.

We took the tube to St. Paul's, an area we had known well in our past, and walked down past our beloved cathedral and then across the Millennium bridge to the Tate Modern. It was the first time we had both seen either place since their opening, and we were both filled with a sense of adventure. After a brief look around the gallery (I never did quite get Modern art, but the building was lovely) we walked along the South Bank, as far as the pedestrian footbridge to the Embankment, stopping to browse in shops along the way, and to look at the book stalls outside the National Film Theatre.

Sometimes I longed to live somewhere other than Dartmoor, and when I spent time with Charlotte that weekend, it felt like an escape, as if I really lived in the metropolis, and life was different. I liked the sense of make-believe, and I could imagine a life where I did lunch with my friends and went shopping at John Lewis whenever I pleased.

Somehow, that day we managed to talk more freely than I remember us talking before. I was at a place in my life where I could finally have fun and enjoy myself despite the crippling bouts of rheumatoid arthritis that would sometimes strike me down, and Charlotte was a lot more relaxed than I had ever seen her. She was just recently home from an acting job that had taken her around the Home Counties being part of a high energy performance of her favourite Shakespeare play in schools, and it had done her the world of good. She was relaxed, confident, and had a glow about her that felt I did not see nearly enough.

I remember it being a magical day which would thankfully be repeated more frequently from then on. Gone were the tense silences, and the petulant glances. Instead I saw that my little girl was growing up at last. She had met a new boyfriend, Stephen, and things were going well.

For me it marked the start of a golden age in our relationship. She felt as if I no longer judged her harshly, and I felt the barriers that had previously been between us melting away.

Funny how perceptions often get in the way of perfectly good relationships; they build these imaginary barriers between us and we spend so much time trying to look around or above them, that we forget that they are just smoke and mirrors. And yet when you prick them with a pin, they disappear with barely a hiss, and all that is left is clean air and the ability to see things more clearly.

So much time is spent in trying to side-step imaginary barriers that just don't exist. But if we can be brave enough to ask questions, and listen to the answers and speak or own truth quietly and clearly, those barriers seem to disappear in a puff of smoke, never to return again, unless we stop listening that is. The surest way to build a barrier is to stop being aware of those around you and start to focus in on yourself, and listen only to your own voice, and your own needs. That is how the illusion of separation is built. Stop talking and listen for a moment and you might just learn something.

That weekend was the first time I had met Stephen in the flesh. I had heard all about him from Charlotte, about the work he did and the fact that he worked with troubled people, like I had, and I looked forward to seeing who this man was who made my daughter blush coyly when she mentioned his name. Stephen was born in England, and his family was Nigerian. I pushed things rather as within an hour of settling in for coffee at his flat, I asked him,

"So what do your friends think of you having a white girlfriend?"

There was a stunned silence for a moment, and then he took a deep breath and took my question by the horns and answered me. He told me that his friends were alright with it, but that if they hadn't been it would not have mattered to him. He could have been offended. He could have thought I was an interfering old bag, who should keep her nose out, the archetypical nightmare of a mother-in-law, but on the contrary, from that day on we got on like a house on fire, and I know we both had a lot of time for each other.

So you see, speaking plainly and not being afraid can free us from so many of our imagined restrictions, from so many of our illusory rules and false limitations. If you can just be brave enough to take a deep breath and ask the questions which are just aching to pop out of your head and leap into the air, then the dance of life and love and humanity can really take flight and flourish.

And what a dance it is when you allow it the freedom to be.

Forty Three

Thursday 14th April 2005

Dear Mum,

My first birthday without you, and at best my odds are to have at least another thirty or so without you. When I put it like that, it feels a frighteningly long time, and yet you did it. You stayed here for thirty-odd years after grandma left you, and yet to me it seems like an interminably long time, too long.

Well, I tried the counselling like people said I should. What a load of crap. I spent the first half hour howling inconsolably, and the counsellor just didn't know what to do with me. I would like to give her the benefit of the doubt and assume bereavement is not her thing, but when I asked her to tell me how sessions with her would be structured, she looked blank and didn't know what to say. All she could suggest was that I wrote you a letter. Silly cow. At one point she even used the clichéd "And how does that make you feel?" That was my final cue to know she was no good and that I needed to get the hell out of there.

Now I am at a loss as to what to do. If a counsellor can't help me, where am I to turn?

And yet again, it is just one more problem I have, one more area in my life where I am at a loss and I know the only person that could give me a decent answer is you.

Love,
XX

Forty Four

9th May 2005

Dear Ma,

It has been a while since I last wrote. Somehow for a while there I got bogged down in the whole pointlessness of everything. Even life seems pointless sometimes when all we have to look forward to is death. So I stopped writing.

But then today, I thought "What if, just imagine if...." Just imagine if you could be looking over my shoulder and reading these words as I place them on the page. Or, what if you could look out through the eyes that you gave me, and feel the things I feel with the emotions you gave me. Hear the music I listen to that makes me think of you. What if...?

So here I am, back with the pen and the blank page, and a heart full of pain and a soul full of fear. Telling you how empty this all is without you seems like a lie. Life goes on regardless, and I must go with its flow, go on or give up and join you. But somewhere in the very belly of my soul, I believe that I am here for a reason; that you should not have struggled so hard to give me life only to have me throw it away ungraciously. That would be unfair. I also believe that we each choose the life we are born into, that I chose to come here and have you be my mother. What a blessing that was, even if I lost you too soon.

For a long while since you became ill, I have fallen out of love with life. I wanted a trial separation or even a divorce, but a voice in my head, that I ultimately think is your voice, tells me that I must go on. That I must learn to love life again, for what good is a half life full of resentment? Surely that would just be a one way ticket to becoming Miss Haversham. I know better than that.

So what good remains in life? What is so good about being here? Chocolate mousse. The smell of the trees after the rain. Jim Morrison, roasted parsnips, raw carrots, and English strawberries. Sunlight glinting on water, waves crashing against the shore. A new outfit worn for the second time, a new haircut a week after it was first done, snow crunching under fur-lined winter boots. Blue paint spread on a white canvas. Fresh jasmine blossom. Fresh mint tea with lots of sugar.

See, all the ways I have to convince myself that life is good even without you.

XX

Forty Five: Violet

Meg is right you know. The separation between us all is just an illusion. That is one of the first myths they dispel when you arrive here. We are all one, part of the same whole, the Collective Unconsciousness, Jung called it. The Islamic tradition has a wonderful analogy that they call the Well of Souls. It is here that the souls of the dead gather and wait for the last judgement, if you believe in the notion of the last judgement. If you go to the Well of Souls and listen, you will hear the voices of all your ancestors, or rather everyone who has ever lived. For your ancestors are my ancestors since we are one and the same, and when you can tap into all of the lessons that all of those people learned, and really learn something from them, there is immense power in that.

Similarly, other traditions talk of the Akashic Records, that somewhere there is an immense storehouse of all the sensations and memories from all existence, all carefully gathered up and placed there to be leafed through with reverence and respect, to be experienced and learned from, because without these ideas, life would seem meaningless. You may pass your genetic coding down to your children and grandchildren, but that constitutes only one tiny fraction of existence. If the unconscious mind processes two million bits of information per second, that information has to go somewhere, it has to mean something, and be of use to somebody, because otherwise all of our struggling and all of the challenges we undergo in physical life would be meaningless, and futile. And the truth is; life may be challenging, but it is never futile.

And the thing is, the Akashic Records are a fascinating place to visit. When I first visited, I was so overwhelmed that I didn't know where to start, so I didn't really start anywhere. I just stood on the outside, completely overawed and paralysed by the enormity of what I was seeing. But after a while, I started to just dip in and out at whim, and not try to tackle all of it, for who could? It is a bit like trying to go round the British Museum, the Victoria and Albert and the Natural History Museums all in one day and look in every single display case and every square inch of space. You could never do it all in one day without full sensory overload and extremely tired feet. The Akashic Record is very like that, but on an infinitely larger scale. It is best appreciated by taking it one little piece at a time. You could spend a million lifetimes in there and not even scratch the surface. But anything you could possibly imagine you want to know about? It is all there ready for you and waiting for the curiosity of the learner to uncover it.

It is one of the highlights of being on this side, of which there are many. There is something very soothing about walking through the hallways, hearing the hushed sounds of the other people around you as they move about the place in quiet reverence. Stand somewhere like the Great Court, or in a busy place like Liverpool Street Station and quieten your own thoughts for a moment and just listen. You will get that same sense of purposefulness, of people going about their lives with a sense of where they are going and what they are going to see. That same sense of peace permeates the hallways and rooms at the Akashic Records. And yet from time to time the quiet will be interrupted by the sound of laughter, as someone relives and shares another person's memories of a joke, or the moment that made a person cry. All human dramas are there to be replayed at will, and all moments of comedy can be enjoyed again and again, but not with the same sense of stuffiness you would find in a physical library. In my younger days as a girl it would always tempt me to do a cartwheel or two, and bang a book down hard on a desk; anything to break the tense silence and shake things up a bit.

But in the Akashic Records there is reverence without repression. There is sensitivity and there is respect. But there

113

is also a great sense of learning, where the subjects that have provided the learning are loved unconditionally, and truthfully. And above all else, there is a strong sense of magic in the air.

Forty Six

27th May 2005

Dear Mumsie,

It is nearing the six month mark, and it is not getting any easier. My good friend at work lost his Mum ten years ago. He tells me that even now, if someone mentions her he dissolves into tears. So maybe I am not abnormal. Maybe I will never "get over this" but simply learn to live with it.

I still feel as if there is a steel band strapped tightly around my chest, digging into the flesh under my arms. If I take a deep breath, and think of you, I feel a sharp pain in my rib cage.

Winter has turned into spring, and spring has turned into summer and still you are not here. It is almost easier to pretend that you are still here, than it is to face the prospect that you are gone for good. To think of you answering the phone with an "alright old girl?" or pottering around in your kitchen. We violate that space that was yours with a sigh, but still you echo "Get out of my kitchen" through our hearts!

I think I could commit murder if it meant I could have you back for the full length of a life. To have another ten or twenty years of you in the world I would choke the life out of a stranger with very little thought.

XX

Forty Seven: Charlotte

I don't feel like I can write anything meaningful anymore. Ok. So I am here. I turned up at the page, like I was supposed to, just like the "How to" creative books said I should. It is stark, and white, and empty. Devoid of all meaning, devoid of language, of pictures, and are you with me? I can't tell.

Nothing. I feel nothing. Maybe it is a blessing. Cool blessed nothingness. A mist descends around me, muffling the sounds of the train through the tunnel. The tick tick of the iPod of the person opposite me, the uncomfortable shuffling of the person standing by my knees. The mist descends, thickening now. Hazy silver cloud through which steps... what? A cow, like at home on the moors? A hansom cab, like in a Sherlock Holmes story? No. Myself. Out of the mist steps me. Tired, distracted-looking, hair dry at the ends, dark circles under my red eyes. She is I-removed. Strange. I have never seen myself from this angle. I feel strangely detached, as I-removed takes a seat opposite me. So that is the tick tick of the iPod, I can hear it now, the haunting sound of the music lifts and falls, carrying I-removed into another place, far away from the inside of the tube carriage. She can't quite decide where she should go, I-removed. She should be in the here and now, but she keeps getting drawn back into that time of Dantésque infernal madness. Wrapped in our mother's shawl, wearing our mother's ring; her talisman ring she called it, as if that will bring her back to physicality. As if anything will bring her back, clinging in a nail-breaking, tearing of the soul kind of way, I-removed sits on the tube, but holds our mother's hand again in her mind, whispering soothing words in her left ear, heads pillowed together as our Mother's breath labours on towards nothingness.

I-removed's eyes fill and spill over, while people around her pretend not to notice the quiet sniffling, the surreptitious dabbing of the damp hanky. I never could stand to see another person cry, and I too start to weep.

Over and over again this scene replays itself, I-removed's mind replaying the last scene over and over again. She thought that was the end point, when our mother was so ill and in such discomfort. At least Death would remove her suffering, at least she would no longer feel the pain, or the discomfort, or the endless retching. At least then our mother could rest.

But what I-removed hadn't bargained for was that our mother's death would not just be an ending, it would also be the beginning of a whole new level of suffering. Nothing had prepared her for that. She had not allowed for the fact that she would no longer sleep at night, and night after night would be laying awake, silent tears streaming onto her pillow. Now she is afraid of the dark, afraid that she will see our mother hovering over her bedside in an eerie phosphorescent light, whilst also wishing it could be so. She hadn't bargained for the fact that her first waking thought and her last conscious thought would be one of excruciating pain, not of the physical kind, that would have been easier to bear. There is no ibuprofen for the soul.

Ah! Poor I-removed. If she were a dog she might have been put out of her misery long ago. But instead she plods on for want of any better ideas, dressed from head to toe in funeral black, long after the event has passed. She is Miss Havisham for our mother, alone, cold, and dreary, full of sharp angry barbs that barely show but are there nonetheless, waiting to fire a dart at anyone who dares to cross her path, desperate to share her pain with someone, even just a little bit.

The train pulls in at a station and the doors open. The mists swirl in air currents, dancing around the sliding doors in a wave. More people step onto the train and sit down. Then the dull thud of the doors closing; and the mists swirl in the opposite direction. The carriage becomes louder as it is now filled with more people. My eyes scan the row of people opposite, past I-removed in the veil of her sorrow, and fall upon another group of figures occupying the seats to the left of I-removed.

Here sits I-who-will-never-be, cradling her four year-old daughter on her lap, while next to her sits our mother, holding a baby. Our mother looks proud, totally wrapped up in the child, attending to his every sound and movement. I-who-will-never-be and our mother talk with ease in a language that requires no words. There is a beautiful lightness to them; they are enjoying their existence, but not with the frivolousness of the unconcerned. They know life's harshness, and enjoy their time together. They laugh over a shared joke, their faces both marked with the same characteristic expressions. Our mother's granddaughter begins to grizzle, over-tired and irritable. Her voice lifts in a wail of "Mummy" and I-who-will-never-be smoothes her hair and kisses the top of her head.

I-removed sitting next to them tries not to cry at the scene, teeth gritted, jaw tightly clenched, she watches I-who-will-never-be out of the corner of her eye, distressed at the sight but unable to draw herself away.

The words run off the page in a blur of liquid and the mists descend once more.

Forty Eight: Violet

If we are extremely lucky, and if we have lived and loved well, when we lose a loved one, what we mourn most is the future not the past. The past will always be there to comfort us, just the space of a thought away, and the future is that intangible thing that hasn't quite materialised yet but exists as a series of dreams and wishes and plans. It is the world of "what if," the world of "if only I could." This is where the true pain lies, because when we live in linear thinking, death comes along and severs the cord with the future, and all we can do is torture ourselves with futures that will never be. In truth, time is not linear, but a lot of physical life is built around this idea that there is a straight line drawn between the past, the present and the future. You are not encouraged to step off that line or deviate; you must fix your eyes on the horizon and keep moving forwards. And yet the truth is so much simpler than that; there is no past and there is no future, only a series of nows. All that ever exists is now.

Granted, this linear time line is a very Western idea; other cultures do not feel the same need for such fixed thinking, but while you live on this very straight road, you live more for the future, and less in the present. What you might have, what you won't have, what you want to have and not what you have now. When our list of possibilities is cut short or taken away, we feel cheated, victimised, disempowered, and helpless as the proverbial newborn baby. "This time next year" stops you from committing to the now, it stops you from taking stock of the current harvest.

The Buddhists encourage their followers to live in the "now" for a very good reason. When you exist in a simple paradigm of "what I have now" things become simple and far more satisfactory. This moment as I write, this moment as I look at a flock of birds flying through the sky in an amazing

V-formation, this moment as I look at the daffodils bobbing their heads in the spring sunshine, and the leaves shimmer in the breeze, this moment as I lie back in a warm bath, this moment I am happy and content and want for nothing.

But since the future is something that is not fixed, since it is something that can't be pinned down or depended upon, it is foolishness to follow the straight line. There may be certain opportunities that are meant to come your way, but ultimately we are given free will to choose to take them or not to take them. "Fate" is too simplistic, and you may as well abdicate all responsibility for your own life, if you decide to take that road and assign "Fate" as being responsible for every little thing that happens. It is a barren dusty road through a desert, with nothing to learn or nourish your soul except the odd shimmering mirage that fails to materialise, when you get up close.

We are given free will for a reason, and it should be exercised as often as possible. You could choose the path through the mountains to free will and a real sense of the spiritual world. The path may be steep and full of stones to trip you up, but the countryside around you is full of life, and gives you plenty to look at and enjoy, and when you get to the top, there is a hell of a view, spreading down the mountain to the valley below and on to the sea, glittering in the sunlight through a slight haze of heat.

This is the path Charlotte has been travelling. She is part-way up the mountain but she feels like a great dark fog has descended and hidden the summit. Just now she wonders if someone has taken the summit away. The path appears to stop dead and she thinks it is the end of the road, but whenever you climb a mountain, you must be ready for the false summits, those plateaux that just before you reach them make you think you are about to reach the top, yet as you come over the brow of the hill you realise there is still some way to go. Just one more push and you will get there.

Charlotte is lost in the mist, and for now she must stop trying to battle with it. She must sit down on a rock and learn to see through the mist to what is around her, to adjust her eyes so she can see what may be hidden from plain sight. Once she can appreciate what is around her again, she will be able to move on, but it may take some time before that can happen, years even.

We choose to experience the physical life for a reason, because we have things we want to learn, things we want to try out, the things we want to experience; the contrasts of light and dark. Duck out of this and you will miss the learning, and may only have to come back around and do it all again. It is better and more constructive to just keep plugging away at it because somewhere amidst all the dirt, there are diamonds glinting in the dark.

Sometimes the dark comes for a reason. It is not by chance that the Egyptian god Osiris was the god of fertility as well as death, and he is not alone. Look at every culture and they have their equivalents. Osiris would cause the Nile to flood and give the land new life; Pele could explode in a fury of molten lava, destroying everything in her path, but forming new land and new islands in the process. Hades, Persephone and Demeter would also play out their annual dance of life and death, summer and winter, while Shiva dances his dance of eternal creation and destruction, creating with one foot and destroying with the other. Adonis dies and where his drops of blood fall flowers spring up, just as Mithras slays a bull and all of nature springs up from beneath them.

The green shoots of new life will appear in Charlotte's life too, but for now all she can see is the flood of steaming lava. Once the water floods the land, fertility will return again. Near our home on the moors, farmers would deliberately burn great stretches of the moors in order to create fertile ground. Once the fire has cleansed the moor of the old heather and gorse, things may look bleak and charcoal-bare, but it will not be long before the new shoots of green will spring to life again.

It is as it should be; an eternal never ending cycle of birth, life and death. The wheel turns ever onwards.

Forty Nine

26th June 2005

Dear Mother,

It is a month since I last wrote to you. Today I am meeting with the rest of my friends to celebrate Midsummer on Hampstead Heath. I have a piece of poetry to share with them as instructed, (I have chosen one of my beloved Shakespeare's sonnets, the one about the glorious Sun, which seems fitting for Mid Summer) and I will buy food in Hampstead for our picnic. All I am missing is a list of blessings for which I am grateful for. Hmmmm. In no particular order of precedence:

I am grateful for Dad. I am grateful he has the strength and the interest in life to keep going, even though he is alone. I am grateful he is my friend as well as my father. I am grateful he has decided to stay with us for a good while longer.

I am grateful for my sister, Ann, for our loyalty, our synchronicity, our femininity, and our unquestioning unconditional love for each other. I am grateful for my brother James who steadies me when I wobble and can give me a different and contrasting view of the world.

I am grateful for my newer friends at the bookshop. I am glad I have somewhere I can go to keep learning. It is a gift that will last me a lifetime.

I am grateful for my skills as an artist and all the things I am good at: writing, acting, painting, brewing. For my means of expression that can be shared with the rest of the world.

I am grateful for my job, that I can be a useful member of society, that I can make a contribution.

Most of all things, I am so utterly grateful that I have had thirty one wonderful years in the presence of my mother. I am grateful for the warmth and caring that she gave me, for what better foundation could I have in life? She gave me my body, my life, my will, my ambition, my humour, my compassion, my love of life, my curiosity, my openness, my reason, my dysfunction, my everything.

Lots of love,
XX

Fifty

4th July 2005

Dear Mumsie,

Life feels so hard at the moment without you. I can't imagine how this will ever get any easier. This weekend coming, I have a wedding to go to (how can anyone celebrate anything?) and then my friend Raven and I are teaching our first workshop on Sunday. Today I had to go out to find an outfit for the wedding, except that I feel fat and frumpy, ugly and soiled, and my favourite (and only) wardrobe advisor has had to move on to new things. Nothing looks or feels right.

The weekend was spent preparing for the workshop, but now I feel strangely calm and have re-assured Raven that we will be ok. I am sure that by Sunday I will be feeling like I need to chain smoke and swig back the whiskey (you will be pleased to know I have stayed off the fags since November now.)

Anyway, I miss you more than anyone should <u>have</u> to miss anyone else.

XX

Fifty One

6th July 2005

Dear Mother,

I am having a scientific day, that being one where I lift up my feelings, turn them over and around and examine them from every angle.

I realised when I walked to the tube that I have entered a totally unfamiliar landscape. I am more isolated than ever before; I watch the stampede of people as if from a distance and I feel totally deserted. And conversely, I can't wait to die.

There are parts of my life that I love; I still enjoy some aspects of living, and I feel infinite love for those who are close to me, and yet when I imagine my own death, all I feel is an overwhelming sense of relief. I can't explain it. It doesn't make me want to reach for the sleeping pills, but I long to give up the struggle.

I wonder why that is? When I held your hand and stroked your hair, and whispered a description of where you were going in your left ear as you left us, did I get too close? Did I step too close to the abyss? When the dark lord came to take you, did I linger too long in his presence and become infected with his kiss? Strange how at times like this only a spiritual angle will do. This is what I am pondering this morning.

Love as always,
XX

Fifty Two: Margaret

The Buddhists believe that somewhere in your unconscious mind you know you are going to die approximately nine months before it is due to happen. How apt for it to be nine months for the gestation of death as well as life, and I say unconscious mind for a purpose; your conscious mind must be totally unaware (for how could you function if it did know) but deep inside yourself you know, and that enables you to get prepared for events.

Looking back I can see some truth in this. I did always believe I would never make old bones. Losing my mother quite early got me prepared for that. I did start collecting the books about cancer, grieving and moving on, and I did find I went almost into hyper drive in the last few years. Whenever we went anywhere, my girls would complain that they couldn't keep up with me as I seemed to do everything at top speed. It was as if I was trying to cram in as much as possible before it was too late.

In life I had just got to the point where I was ready to really start enjoying myself. After a tough time with rheumatoid arthritis in my late forties and early fifties that lead to me having to give up the work that had so inspired me, the medical profession had just got my medication right, and I was beginning to enjoy feeling well again.

My social life was better than I ever remembered, as I had finally found a group of friends that enjoyed the same things as me, and overall we just had so much fun together. My special friend Ruth brought such lightness to my life, she was a great gift to me, and yet we could still talk about things of immense substance. There were dinners and garden parties, conferences and charity work. There were holidays and warm days in the sun, adventures abroad and lots of new people to meet and learn from. My life really sparkled in the last four years, so much so that when my friends asked me at a party one night, "Well, Margaret, if you could change anything in your life, what would it be?" in all honesty and sincerity, I immediately replied, "Not a single thing."

When I started to notice the symptoms of the cancer it was subtle at first. I actually thought I had indigestion, but after a few weeks of it not going away, I started to get an inkling that something was not right. When my family look back on the photos of the last holiday we had at Loch Lomond in September, now they notice a slight puffiness around my face they never noticed before. Stupidly my doctor at the time told me to take ibuprofen, but neglected to mention that this should only be for four days. After several weeks I went back and they finally began to listen and start doing tests. By November I was really feeling it; pain in my stomach and a deep feeling of discomfort under my rib cage.

Could they have caught it earlier and done something? I don't think so. Unfortunately they can't do much about the pancreas, and my oncologist would later tell my husband Martin that he had never in all his life encountered a more aggressive tumour. This was an unmistakable, unshakable "please leave by the nearest exit" announcement that came loud and clear over the tannoy. To say I was annoyed would be an understatement. There was so much I still wanted to experience in life, so much I still wanted to do, but how do you fight nature at the end of the day? Some things you just have to accept.

We all have to go sometime. Our bodies are biological animals that can only serve us for a certain amount of time, and although we all know this in our hearts, mostly we manage to suppress that realisation, and act as if it is not really so. But when somebody sits across a desk from you and has to tell you it is not only imminent but only a matter of a few weeks away at the most, it is quite a different kettle of fish.

I have to say my first reaction was to feel sorry for the doctor for having to deliver this piece of news. But then I will confess I kept it hidden for a couple of weeks. It was Martin's birthday soon after and stupidly or not, I felt I didn't want to ruin it for him, not just that year but for every year afterwards. I didn't want him to spend every birthday from then on associating it with that news. So I stalled the Oncologist, and told no one but Ruth. We managed to keep it under wraps for the time being, and as soon as Martin's birthday had passed, I broke the news.

It was the most painful thing I think I had ever had to say to anyone, and when Martin knew, I then had to call each of the children and tell them too, as I wanted them to hear it from me. Martin sat with me and held my hand while I called them, keeping a very stoic expression on his face despite the turmoil inside.

I felt strangely calm really. I told Charlotte first of all, and she responded with surprising strength, but I know that when she finished the conversation she gave vent to the full strength of her feelings, as did her father and I once we had called Ann and James as well. I agreed with each of them that we needed a day or two just to get our heads around the information before reconvening and thinking about a way forward. The children never asked what happened during those few days, and I would never tell them. Some things are just too personal to share, especially with your children.

I had always said that if I was ever diagnosed with cancer that I would opt for no treatment at all. I had witnessed my own mother, and many other people after her, going through the endless rounds of chemotherapy; the sickness, the weakness, the loss of hair, and the loss of dignity just scared me really. But when it actually came down to it, for the sake of my dear ones, I felt I had to at least try.

So the endless visits to the hospital began, and I was poked and prodded and fussed over. I would come out of the hospital, go home and be unable to keep anything down, including water, and then, dehydrated, I would be readmitted and put on a drip. Finally, after several weeks in which the doctors became increasingly horrified at the speed in which it took over and laid waste to all in its path, the cancer won. At the end of November it was thought that I had a good chance of surviving for six months. By the time Christmas began its final approach, it was very clear that this was not so.

One day as I sat in the hospital waiting for my Oncologist with Charlotte and Martin, we finally made up our minds. After a particularly painful procedure in which the doctors had tried to put in a stent to enable my liver to function, I knew in my heart that we were fighting a losing battle. Martin sat in a chair beside the bed, and Charlotte sat on the end of the bed while I propped myself up on my pillows.

Two beds down an old lady lay behind a curtain making the final journey over the threshold. We could hear her laboured breathing, and tried not to disturb her and her daughter by speaking in low tones.

"What do you think?" I asked them both. Martin and Charlotte both thought for a moment, then Martin said,

"Never mind what we think, what do you want to do?"

I shrugged, and Charlotte continued,

"If you want to fight this out, then we will fight it out. But if you have had enough and are just putting on a brave face for our benefit, then I think you should say. If you have just had enough of being poked about and prodded and want to just go home and batten down the hatches, then we are with you. Whatever you want is fine, as long it is what you really want and not what you feel obliged to do for our benefit."

I smiled a wry smile at them both. At this point a cry rang out from behind the curtain. The old lady had slipped away and her daughter started to sob, while a nurse tried to comfort her. I looked over at Charlotte and saw the strangest thing. She sat with her eyes closed, and an expression I can only describe as one of immense peace on her face. I knew that she was somehow sensing the old lady, and that everything was alright for her now. I asked Charlotte if this was so, and she smiled and nodded.

"I don't know how or why," she said, "but I felt her in the room and she seemed happy and was somehow telling me she is ok now. She *felt* as if she looked really well."

Somehow, although none of us could explain this experience, or even wanted to try, it made the decision a lot simpler.

"I think," I said, "that what I would really like to do is just go home for Christmas and be in my own bed."

We drove home that day almost in a state of bliss, although looking back you could wonder what we had to be happy about. The day was bright and sunny, and the colours looked so vivid to me. As we drove along the top road above our house, I looked down and felt a deep sense of peace, for even if this was the last time I would make this journey, I was at least for one last time safely back at home.

The next time I left the house was in an ambulance with Charlotte and Martin, but thankfully by then I had slipped away in my mind, and was not really seeing what was happening. It is a blessing to be able to switch your awareness off sometimes, one of nature's gifts for when things become really hard. I just had to trust the process and have faith that things would be fine. At the final point of life, you reach one last question to which you can never really find a definitive answer before it is time to go; does life just stop, or does some small part of it carry on beyond that final lifting of the veil? Or does some big part of it carry on? For all of us, this can only be a question you can answer by faith, and everybody's conclusion might be different. But you see therein lies our beauty; that each of us create our own reality, and each of us is unique, although we are all the same. It is the great paradox of nature that we seem to spend most of our lives chasing like a phantom in the mist; are we the same or are we different? The beauty of the answer lies in the fact that we are both.

Fifty Three

8th July 2005

Dear Mum,

It happened at last, the thing that I had half been expecting for some time. With all the events around the world it was inevitable really. Yesterday morning during rush hour there were explosions at Edgware Road, Aldgate, Russell Square and on a bus in Tavistock Square. It was weird really; surreal, freakily calm.

I was about two or three tubes behind the Russell Square one. Something exploded between King's Cross and Russell Square. I got as far as Arsenal, only one stop away from home, and the train stopped. The driver said there had been an incident at King's Cross; person under a train we all thought. But we waited, and waited. After a while, the driver said "there has been a serious incident at King's Cross" but he couldn't get radio dispatch to respond. I waited about half an hour, but it was so cramped that my face was squashed against the door, and I had to get in early to work to sort out a training session with a new trainer who was coming in. So I bailed out, got above ground, walked in the direction that I thought was Holloway Road, and thought I would get a bus to work.

I arrived unexpectedly at Blackstock Road, completely the other side of the train tracks than I had thought I would be, and jumped on the first bus I could find. If I could just get into central London I would work it all out from there. Then I sat back and enjoyed the bus ride – Highbury Corner, Upper Street, City Road, and eventually the Barbican, the Museum of London and St. Paul's Cathedral.

Then the passengers started to talk around me as rumours started to circulate, and it started with "train crash", then "gas leaks". Odd. So I checked the Internet on my phone, and it said there were power surges in three or four stations leading to explosions. Great. But then just past St. Paul's the bus stopped, and all the passengers were thrown off, rather unceremoniously I thought, and in the middle of nowhere, and not even at a bus stop. But hey ho, I thought, there is a coffee shop; I will stop for a coffee and a loo break at least. I chatted to a lady in the queue about the strange goings on and then set off to walk down Fleet Street in the direction of work, thinking that if no train or bus would take me there, then I would bloody well walk if I had to.

I walked on until I reached Kingsway, and stopped off at Smiths, where the staff were all of a flutter, a bus had exploded somewhere, and all the networks were down; no trains, no buses, no tubes, nothing. And then I started to get scared, because as I walked up Kingsway towards the office, all the mobile networks went down, and people were huddled around the window of an electrical shop, watching the TV screens. It looked like a scene from a disaster movie, and I half expected Godzilla to come around the corner.

The office was chaos; one of the bosses was just leaving, and one of the women was all in a panic, asking me to have a look at her laptop, which I tried to do, I am not sure why, especially as it is not even my job anymore. Then she got all impatient to leave, and couldn't I hurry up? I interrupted an update, and got the blue screen of death. I buggered up the laptop, and that is all I can think of now.

The phones were ringing non-stop. Worried spouses, partners and family members all trying to track down their loved ones. My boss was unaccounted for and his family were understandably having kittens, while I just kept trying to fix the fucking laptop. By midday, my boss strolled in, oblivious to the panic at home, and things started to calm down a bit, while I still stressed over the laptop. By now the phone systems were intermittently dropping out, there were

132

no mobiles, no Internet access, and no digital radio. Why the hell hadn't I just turned back at Arsenal?

Enough was enough, we all decided. Let's all concentrate on getting home. So we left at about half past two, and four of us set out on foot, heading for Finsbury Park. We got turned back at Russell Square, turned back at King's Cross, and eventually we made our way up Grey's Inn Road towards Angel. At the Angel, we stopped to buy a sandwich and then headed down Liverpool Road, up Hornsey Road (past the new Arsenal Stadium) through the estates and then home.

I got home at about four o'clock, ate lunch, watched the news, spoke to every friend I haven't heard from for months and then dozed off.

Now it is two in the morning, and I can't sleep. Someone rang here at midnight.

What else can I say?

XX

Fifty Four: Violet

It is sad that a human can kill another human in the name of religion, and yet more wars have been started over religious views than for land, and from where I am I can see it is all futile. Everyone fighting for their viewpoint to be right, but what is so frightening about being wrong once in a while? You might actually learn something if you can show enough humility to accept that there are other viewpoints, which are just as valid, and there is another way. But the human animal does not appear to be built to fall easily into a state of humility, without hard work to get there, and a lot of risk-taking. It is silly really. Being wrong is not so bad. Ah! The human ego – always insisting on defending its own position, even beyond the point where it has stopped believing it is even right anymore, just as long as it doesn't have to back down and admit it may have been wrong.

As Stephen and his friends were so fond of saying to Charlotte, "Same bush, different way round it," and they were right. The bush is the same awe-inspiring magnificent bush that it ever was, call it God, Allah, Goddess, Spirit, Jehovah, Ganesh, Shiva, Hecate, Isis, Osiris, whatever you call it, it is just as beautiful and it inspires all of us to create with it. Inspiration literally means the breath of God, and that is no accident. I once heard a very wise man say that God is simply a creation by humans trying to grasp the awe inspiring-nature and the magnificence of the infinite. He did not say this to diminish it, rather to demonstrate the vastness, and the diversity of it. Whatever *It* is, words do not do It justice.

It does not want us to kill, torture or maim each other, although as Sekhmet, Kali or Pele it may display a certain bloodlust. And yet humans will kill themselves and others, all in the name of religion, and religion is man's ideas about what God wants. I never would have thought in life that I would have learned to speak what some people would call heresy. I attended church regularly, and it was a Baptist Church, but the views I have now don't diminish what I felt and believed then; they have just added to it.

On a day like the one in London, where people were killing people in such a sad display of misconceived notions of the nature of God, things get very busy around here, for those facing mortal danger or death never face it alone. Just now Margaret has been helping a young man who was on the train at Edgware Road when one of the bombs went off. He is lying in hospital, having lost all feeling in the lower part of his body and the sight in one eye, wondering what the point of living is when he will spend the rest of his life dependent on his loved ones for care and getting around. This was a fit and healthy young man who used to love running, and now that has been taken away from him simply because he happened to be in the wrong place at the wrong time, but Margaret will guide him and watch over him just as patiently and as generously as she watched over those less fortunate than her when she was living. Another of our soul group has been watching over a young woman who had just lost her mother in the weeks before the bombing. Her father, like Charlotte's father, will have had the absolute terror of not knowing what has happened to his daughter in the few hours of chaos, which followed the explosions. He will have been relatively lucky this time as she was hurt but not killed. But they will cling to each other in the next few months, afraid for each other constantly. Charlotte will watch them on the news and be moved by their story, so close is it to hers, and feel so lucky for her family at least that she managed to stay away from the main places of violence. "There but for the grace of God go I", she will think, as will Martin and Ann and James when they find out just how close she was to what happened, and thousands of others just like them. Charlotte's journey was no accident. She had many people from our side ensuring that she was kept away from danger.

Martin, so deeply affected by the experience of thinking he may have lost someone else so soon after he lost Margaret, will make Charlotte promise faithfully that she will not die before him, and she will agree to it, shaken by the idea of the pain it would inflict on him. That is a promise that will come back to haunt Charlotte in her darkest moments, but it is one which will possibly save her from harming herself, or giving up and deciding to come home for good. And we will keep supporting her, silently, watchfully and lovingly.

Those on the physical plane may not be able to see those of us who help them, but we are there guiding, consoling, giving them the strength to take just one more breath, just one more step towards life. How sad that in the physical world we often feel so alone, so lonely, and yet you are never alone. Never.

Fifty Five

14th July 2005

Dear Mum,

Stress stress stress! A busy week of meetings and
problems and so much to do it is inhuman! I have broken that
woman's laptop, and tomorrow she will find out all her files
are gone because she didn't back them up and THAT is not
my fault, and yet somehow it always feels like my fault. Why
can't I be myself around this person? She brings out the worst
in me and I am not sure why, I could have been just like her. I
don't like her way of interacting with the world, but
somehow I always feel I need her approval. Why? *Why?* It
doesn't make any sense at all.

And I so wanted to sleep like a baby tonight. I am worried
about Dad being on his own, I am worried about James, I
worry about Ann, and sometimes I feel like no one worries
for me.

On Tuesday I was at our drop-in at work, and a client
brought in a tiny baby, a wee little thing. It turned out it
wasn't hers, but she rescued it from a crack house. Fucking
hell. And I think I have problems? That poor little mite is
barely two months old, and what has she ever done to deserve
that? Bombs going off, babies in crack houses, the whole
world has gone mad. It just doesn't make any sense to me.
Oh Mumsie, Mumsie, Mumsie. Somehow, it always feels like
you are the only person who could help me to make sense of
the world.

XX

Fifty Six: Violet

Poor dear Charlotte getting so bogged down in the unnecessary details at the moment. One day she will look back on this and wonder what the fuss was about with broken laptops, but for now there are too many spinning plates and too many things to juggle, when her thought processes are already so muddled and confused. Part of the problem with depression is that there is just too much around you for you to see clearly, there is too much unnecessary packaging wrapped tightly around your life for you to be able to discern what you really need to focus on. It drags you down, and the further you descend into the abyss, the harder it becomes to claw your way out again.

And the anti-depressants won't help you either. Thankfully Charlotte has not taken that particular get-out clause; for if you can't cope with life without anti-depressants you certainly won't be able to cope with it with them. They numb your senses and stop you from being able to think clearly. They interfere with the delicate chemicals in your brain, and stop you from being able to connect, which can only make things worse when it is the sense of connection that may have led you to feel this way in the first place. Charlotte has a very dear friend who has cautioned her against them, and I am glad for that. Her friend will tell her one day of a visit she once made to a doctor to talk about depression. She was prescribed the pills which she duly took, but on her second visit to the GP, with her thoughts, reactions and feelings clouded accordingly, as she sat in front of the doctor's desk, gazing through the window behind the doctor at the nice little garden outside, a fox suddenly appeared at the window, its paws balanced up on the window sill, its eyes peering into the room. Charlotte's friend jumped at the sight, but the doctor, oblivious to the scene behind her continued to

138

write out the prescription and talk in a monotonous voice about how long to take the medication for.

Charlotte's friend never made it as far as the chemist; she was not sure if the fox was real or imagined, but the uncertainty was enough to put her off anti-depressants for life. Charlotte is lucky to have good friends around her who are willing to share their own experiences, and the ability to learn by the lessons of others without feeling the need to experience those things for herself.

Sticking your fingers into the heart of the hungry, angry flames is not the only way to learn that fire will burn you.

Fifty Seven

17th July 2005

Dear Mum,

Sometimes I seem to muddle along in a la la state of being, but then all of a sudden, little glimpses of where my soul lies bleeding impose themselves on my conscious mind. Brief thirty second glimpses becoming louder and louder, until I can barely hear myself think. I can't even bear to wail, it is so utterly deep and gut-wrenching, whole and familiar, and my mother has gone. I have never before known a pain as utterly wrenching as this, and wholly without relief of any kind.

All I seem to feel these days is negativity, and I hate it. I hate being this depressed, this thoroughly pissed off at life, so that I can't actually see a single reason worth living for. If I could, I would rather die, but after the bombing I promised Dad I would not go before him. He was so scared it had been me, as it was my tube line, and my bus route to work, he was worried they would have got me either way. So he made me promise not to die before him, and now I am contracted to stay here, at least until he leaves.

Somehow I know that the gods have not finished with me yet. There is still something they want me to do, but for the life of me I have absolutely no idea what it is and I wish they would hurry the fuck up with it, because this is just horrendously bad. It is like watching a really bad film, or reading an excruciatingly bad book, but somehow you are not allowed to leave before the end or stop reading; you just have to get on and finish it, even if it means sitting there in excruciating pain or numbness, because your bum has gone to sleep.

I miss you more than I can say, Mum. And I feel so alone. As if I don't have anyone in the world. I miss being nurtured, having someone who cares about me because I feel like all I do is care about other people and get nothing in return, and all the while everyone is totally unaware because they never ask me. And all the while rage builds inside of me, waiting to boil over. And if I could, I would trade all of this for just one more week with you, and then that makes me feel worse because I am also a wicked nasty person for feeling that way.

Maybe I am bad. Maybe I am suffering from depression and I should rethink and ask my doctor for anti-depressants. Or maybe I am just grieving the loss of my favourite person. Who knows? I certainly don't any more.

And I don't want to send you any more poison. You are not supposed to send people you love letters like this. I just sound like another one of your lame ducks.

XX

Fifty Eight: Margaret

Cancer of the pancreas is a real bugger. Of all the forms of cancer you could possibly have, this one is the most deceitful, insidious and sneaky. It creeps in silently under the cover of darkness and starts to work away at you, deep inside you under your rib cage where most tests can't even go. By the time you start to exhibit the symptoms; the weight loss, the puffiness, the pain, it is too late to do anything about it. They can't remove your pancreas, and you cannot get a transplant. Treating it is extremely difficult, and the most the chemotherapy will give you (if you are well enough to have chemotherapy- I wasn't) is a few more weeks to live. One in six people live for another year, but most people never make it past a year. Some like me don't even make it past a second month.

One way or another, when you have pancreatic cancer, you are on your way out. It is just a matter of how long. It's the one Nature gives you when she doesn't expect an argument, you just have to go along with her, be accepting and hope that she won't give you too hard a time on the way out, that you may pass quietly and quickly on with as little discomfort as possible.

Before we left the hospital to go home, my oncologist told us that it would be possible to do genetic tests on the girls to see if they were likely to get it too. Since Violet and I had both had it, there was a fifty-fifty chance the girls would get it too. Luckily for James at this point, we had adopted him at the age of six months, so he was spared that particular genetic lottery. But I made the girls promise to at least look into having the tests done.

I went with Ann to the genetic research unit at her local hospital to speak with the specialist there. Of course Ann and the specialist had no idea that I was in the room with them, but I wanted to hear what he had to say. It wasn't pretty. Because of the deeply buried location of the pancreas, the tests would be extremely invasive and uncomfortable, and would have to be done at least annually for them to be of any use or meaning.

Ann and Charlotte weighed up the options over the telephone.

"He said it was likely to be a very uncomfortable process," Ann said.

"And what could they do if we did show up as having the likelihood of getting it?" asked Charlotte.

"Well, that is where I am not quite clear," Ann said. "It seemed as if there isn't actually much they can do." There was a slight pause as the girls both digested the information.

"Sounds as if we would be going through the motions every year, experiencing a lot of discomfort only to be told we will die one day. We already know we are going to die one day, so if it is a toss-up between being made to feel uncomfortable every year or to just leave things alone, I think I would rather not bother." Charlotte shrugged and Ann sighed.

"I think we already know everything they could tell us."

"I am not sure," said Charlotte, "that I want someone to tell me when it is going to happen and if it is going to happen. I think I would rather just take the chance and deal with it as and when it arises."

"I think you are right," said Ann. "What's to be gained from knowing? If you know it is coming it will only be there looming on the horizon. I can't imagine anything worse."

"I can't think of anything worse than being told, yes, the likelihood is that you will get pancreatic cancer, but we are not quite sure when exactly. We already know it might be on the cards, what can we gain by knowing for sure, if there is nothing they can do to treat it if you do get it?"

"I wonder what Mum would say?" pondered Ann.

"I'll tell you what I would say; I would tell them where to stick their tests!" I said, but of course they couldn't hear me.

"I think she would tell them where to stick their tests," said Charlotte. That's my girl!

"Yeah. You're right. She would," said Ann, "Just before taking a therapeutic trip to the John Lewis Kitchen department. "

"What did Dad say?" asked Charlotte.

"He said it was up to us, but either way he would support us in any way he can."

"Well, that settles it for me," said Charlotte. "If Dad really wanted us to do it, then I might just go through with it, but if he can see it is a pointless exercise, then I would rather not bother. It is not for me."

"I will try and talk to Dad about it. I think he was worried for us, and just wanted to know that we know what we might be dealing with."

I think my girls are both chips off the old block. It makes me very proud to think they are able to deal with these difficult questions with such grace and dignity. I only wish they could feel me near them, trying to support and give them some strength. But then maybe, just maybe, I am underestimating their talents. I think they do know I am here. I think when they spend time quietly contemplating and trying to find a sense of quiet in their minds, and allowing time for peace to come into their souls, they will feel me there. In the meantime I can't resist just nudging them once in a while to encourage them to feel my presence. It was no accident that pushed our lives together, and in the end it was the natural way of things that meant we had to be apart too. But I am still here with them. And I am not going anywhere too far away from them. Our worlds are closer together than you might think.

Part Three:

Bring Me To Life

Fifty Nine

26th October 2005

Dear Mumsie,

Hello. It is me. I am back again, kind of. I have been away for some time, at least three months I would say. I got fed up with my own moaning. I got swallowed up in my own despair, a dark cloak that wrapped me in its sticky, smelly stench. It got too much, so I just stopped on the page, put the paper to one side and walked away from it. I think I will seal those pages in wax, and bury them somewhere on a lonely hill on the moors, never to be revisited for fear of contamination. You see, despair is catching. It is like a virus that you just can't shake off, and it invades every pore, every cell. Just talking about it brings the old spectre out, looming in its shadow form.

But I learned something about the shadow. You have to learn to look it in the eye and not flinch. The keeper at the gate between the two worlds, the dark lord, you have to look him in the eye. You have to learn to love him, but not be so enthralled that you forget to live as well. Death can be so seductive; I still dream of it, and I still look forward to its release, but I also know I have to learn to live life again too. It is not yet my time to come and join you, not just yet.

My time will come soon enough, but meanwhile, I need to make the best of things here. I need to find some joy in it. I need to love. And I need to live.

XX

Sixty: Margaret

My love, we all applaud you for this decision, most of all me. Because now you have decided to live again, I can start to live again. There are things here that most people cannot imagine. There are things here I have only just begun to imagine myself, but now I can fully embrace all that there is to experience, because I know that we will each be learning new things, we will each be exploring new things, and those things will eventually bring us back together. I can rise up to meet my new adventures, knowing that in your own way, you are rising up too. And knowing this will only make these experiences better for me.

While these experiences will always be tinged with the sadness of separation, they will not be consumed by it. Don't forget my dearest one that you have been with me before and you will be with me again.

The very nature of life is that you are a spiritual being who has gone to have a physical experience. We are all spiritual beings, and this is something we all have in common, although many of us may not realise it in life. It is much easier for someone in the physical world to raise their vibrations up to the spiritual, than it is for someone in the spiritual plane to lower their vibrations down to meet you.

By pledging yourself to carry on, you are also ensuring that we can still be together. Learn to embrace life again and you will embrace me again. Dream of me when you sleep and your dreams will not just be the fantasy of your unconscious mind, they will be soul flights in which we can sit together again and talk about things we are doing. You may not remember when you awake, but part of me will stay with you during the day, nestled closely and carefully in your heart. You will carry me with you, just as I carry you with me. Learn to embrace the infinite, and the voice that calls out to you in your heart will be mine, and your grandmother's, and your great grandmother's, for we are all one and the same, you and I.

In your quietest moments, when you still your racing thoughts and soothe your aching heart, my words can reach across the divide and my love will embrace you. For love is the bond that binds us together and not even Death can sever that link.

Laugh with your friends, and I will laugh with you. We can still enjoy the same jokes we always enjoyed. Sing and dance to our favourite songs and I will sing and dance with you.

Uphold the principles I have taught you and you will in turn inspire others, and then you will keep my name and my memory alive. I am not a construct of your imagination; I may not be flesh and blood but I am alive all the same. Do the things we would have done together and enjoy them just the same, and I will be there by your side, still doing them with you.

But if you languish in fear and in doubt, then my reach is not far enough to touch you. Mourn my passing, but do not mourn the gift of a life we have given you, for it is indeed a gift and you were not brought up to return a gift with no word of thanks. Instead embrace all the experiences life gives you with both hands and an open heart, and I will experience them with you. I can live vicariously through you, for you are mine, and I am yours and we are both joined.

When you sit rooted to the spot with fascination at talks held at your beloved friend's bookshop, marvelling at the mummification techniques in Ancient Egypt, or at the traditional folk magic practices in Transylvania, I will be sitting right beside you, equally as riveted. When you marvel at the beauty of the choir singing Mozart's "Requiem," listen closely because you will be able to pick out my voice distinctly amongst the sopranos in the front row. When you sit and gaze at the Degas "After the Bath" in a gallery full of chattering school children, I will stand next to you and feel your wonder and gain energy from your own inspiration. What feeds your soul will feed mine also and that of everyone around you.

Talk to me as if I was still there, and I will hear you. Listen carefully to the silence that envelops you, and you will hear my thoughts in your thoughts, my words will become your words. Lovey, this is how you can reach me, and it is how you can help me to reach you.

Live your life to the full, experience all that you can, find inspiration and enjoyment in the most mundane and small tasks, and I will learn from them as well. For everything you do will be recorded, and others will benefit also. I have seen that it is so, and one day I will show you round the great halls and courts of the Akashic records, and you will see it also.

And this, my daughter, is all that I wish for you.

Sixty One

28th October 2005

Dear Mum,

The world is shifting, degree by degree, and it is disconcerting.

Dad feels it is time for him to go "back out there" and start meeting people again, meeting women again. We have talked about this a lot, and I think it is a positive sign that he is still interested in life. Potentially he could have many years ahead of him, and I don't think he likes life on his own, which is fair enough. It has divided opinion around us. Is it disloyal to your memory? Is it too soon? I think only Dad can answer that, but I do think it is a sign that at least he is engaging with the business of living again, which surely must be better than engaging with the business of dying, which has been the constant companion of all of us since you left.

I have been reading the Tao te Ching by Lau Tzu and there is a verse that springs to mind that talks about living plants as being green and flexible and dead plants being dry and brittle. Lau Tzu says that therefore the truly wise seek to be flexible as it means they become the disciples of life and not the disciples of death.

I think this is where we are now. We have to learn to adapt to the changes or we all may as well give up now.

But the tricky thing is how do we adapt? That is the key and the secret to this business of living.

Answers on a self-addressed stamped post card please...

Love,
XX

Sixty Two

5th December 2005

Dear Mum,

Time is ticking on. Already on my computer screen there
it is, "Ma's Birthday" and Ma's Deathday soon after it,
looming in my not very distant future. Twenty seven days to
go. Tick tock, tick tock.

I am so tired, and yet tonight I cannot sleep. My skin feels
like a thousand fire ants are biting at it, my chest hurts and I
cannot breathe properly. My life feels like a colossal failure
as everything I have ever wanted to do has not quite come to
fruition. I just wanted to be creative. I just wanted to express
this amazing energy I have inside of me, but now I feel as if it
is turning in on me, eating me alive from the inside out.

I miss you every day. I can't get over the intense pain. I
can't express just how excruciating it is.

James had a psychic reading done which said you are
around me all the time, so why can't I feel you? All I can feel
is the gaping emptiness.

I am locked in this life that hasn't turned out how I
wanted, and I don't know how to be joyous with it anymore.

And I am tired of this moaning fat expensive failure of a
life.

Love,
XX

Sixty Three: Margaret

They say life is just one big fat disappointment until you let go and stop trying to control it. I think the reason I was able to tell my friends in those last months that I wouldn't change a thing, was because I had stopped trying to fight the current and instead had learned to enjoy the gentler pace of drifting along in the flow. I had spent so much of my life fighting something; fighting social exclusion, fighting society's need for the woman to be quiet and docile and be happy with washing her net curtains in suburbia, fighting to bring up my children, fighting rheumatoid arthritis, that by the time the cancer came, I was done with fighting nature, or god or whatever you would label it, and knew it was a futile struggle that would only end in frustration.

And yet when I drifted with the tide, I found only immense peace, when I learned to trust the process I found immense peace. When I asked the powers that be to give me the strength I needed to get through, they gave it to me. I tried to explain this to Charlotte and Martin in the hospital towards the end, and I expected Charlotte to react with shock or derision or for her to think me foolish. But she surprised me when her response was, "Yes, I know what you mean. I pray every day too and I find it really helps."

Perhaps I had assumed she was godless as she did not appear to be following a conventional path, but she held my hand then and with Martin holding my other hand, we had a moment of soul recognition, and a feeling of warmth seeped through me. That steadied me in the next few days as I really knew they were there for me, without hesitation. They would speak for me in the hall of Ma'at if I needed them to. If my heart was to be weighed against a feather, they would vouch for me. Whatever Charlotte's path was, and however different it may have seemed from mine on the outside, it involved looking out for and accommodating the emotional needs of others, which ultimately was what my life's purpose had always been. Our paths were in fact running along parallel lines. Separation and division really are only an illusion.

I wish I could show Charlotte that her life is anything but a failure, but perception is projection; if she thinks it is a failure it will be a failure and a waste of time, as she will not be physically able to see the opportunities as they come along and present themselves. For the moment at least this is a fight that needs to be tackled head on.

A very wise woman[1] once wrote that the plans we make for our own lives are just like the shadows cast by a large tree against the snow. The tree stands against the changing seasons; leaves will uncurl and then fade and die, and the shadow of the tree will change and move with the dancing of the leaves in the breeze. The shadow of the tree will fall against snow, and at other times onto the soft earth, the shadows of the leaves will dance darkly on the ground they will fall onto and leave the branches bare, but throughout all of this, the one thing that remains constant is the tree. I think that sometimes in the physical life we forget we are like the tree and not the shadow it casts, and we get too caught up in thinking about which way the snow is drifting, a detail which we have no control over. We get so caught up in trying to work out which way the path is going, we forget to look up and enjoy the blue skies and the clouds above us, to see the stars and realise the true scale of this life.

There is something far bigger than us at play in the universe; older than the hills and more powerful than the oceans, wider than the stars and deeper than amber, and full of infinite love. Life is really simpler than we give it credit for. Our purpose is usually far simpler than we imagine. But instead we fight the currents we drift in and give ourselves an unnecessarily hard time. We define ourselves by what we own or what we do, and happiness never lies on that path.

Your life is a failure? Compared to what? According to whom? Who says it is a failure? If we spoke to other people using the voice we use in our own thoughts to address ourselves, mostly we would be horrified and we would not tolerate it. So why is it ok to be that harsh on yourself?

In the last few months of my life, I suppose I really tried to be a lot less hard on myself, and my family really helped with that. When I saw the love and tenderness they had for me, I realised I couldn't have done that bad a job. They took me home when all I wanted to do was be in my own bed again. They cared for me as I had cared for them at their beginnings, and they did it without hesitation, without question.

Maybe the only way to judge a life is how well you have loved, and how well you have been loved. When you look around at the people in your life, those you choose to share your life with, what do you see reflected back? Do you see love? Do you see tenderness and caring? Or do you see possessions and wealth and shiny things. Although we may not be able to take any of these things beyond the veil of death, neither possessions nor people, the love that binds us does persist, and does survive the crossing.

I don't think anyone's life is a failure if they have learned to love someone so unconditionally and been so loved in return.

Sixty Four

27th December 2005

Dear Mumsie,

I visited the Museum of London with my friend Raven today. It felt so poignant as I came here not so long ago with you and Ann. We had a sushi picnic on the benches outside, just as you and I and Ann did, and talked long and with ease.

There was so much there to see, and lots to catch up on as Raven had just returned from Spain. We walked all round the museum, taking in with particular interest the pre-historic section, the Suffragettes and the exhibition downstairs from three black photographers recording their own personal histories of growing up in this country.

One of the things I was reminded of was the fact that Ann taught me about the Suffragettes as she did a school project on it. Raven and I agreed that everyone needs someone to teach them these bits of history, as it is our history. We saw the film of Emily Wilding Davison being run down by the King's horse. What a brutal death. We saw the Cat and Mouse poster where the cat holds the limp body of the woman in its mouth, and the picture of the woman being force fed with a tube. And that was only a century ago.

The other highlight was the "Roots to Reckoning" exhibition by Ahmet Francis, Neil Kenlock and Charlie Phillips. It was interesting that all three were brought up by their grandparents and then sent to London to live with their parents around the age of ten or twelve. The themes that really resonated for me were those of a lack of their own history, and also the cultural ideals of beauty. There were pictures of Bob Marley, and Mohammed Ali, and the Black

157

Panthers, but there were also pictures of ordinary people from their communities going about their everyday lives. You would have loved it.

Love,
XX

Sixty Five: Margaret

I remember when the children were very small I used to take them to the Museum of London. While we lived in Devon, Martin worked in London so he lived there most of the time but would come home whenever he could at weekends.

Whenever we would visit him in the city, I would always ask the children where they would like to go first, and they would always give me one of three answers; the museum, Covent Garden, or Hamley's on Regent Street, the enormous toy shop. On some visits to London, it would be hard to dissuade them from visiting the museum every day. I am not quite sure what was the source of such fascination, but it was certainly gripping. We visited so often in fact, that the couple who worked on the information desk knew us by name, and we even went to visit them in their home once when we were up. They were people Martin had known, when he was a boy in primary school.

The part I really had trouble pulling Charlotte away from was the Great Fire of London exhibit. There was a model of London set behind a glass window, and the story of the fire, as recorded in the diary of Samuel Pepys was narrated by Michael Horden. I suppose Charlotte liked it a lot, as she liked Paddington Bear and Michael Horden's voice was the common denominator, but as he reached various parts in the story, little flickering lights would turn on inside the model to indicate the spread of the fire. It was all quite low tech, even in those days, but every time we went I would have to stand behind Charlotte as she reached up to the wooden rail and watched wide eyed and open mouthed and listened to the whole thing all over again.

I suppose now it is a place that acts as a sympathetic link between us both. I stood again with Charlotte as she watched the show today, and I could feel her little heart yearning for those days. Sometimes when you are grieving for someone very dear it is those sympathetic links that give you the only comfort, but even if they are meagre and cold. It is a bit like wanting a roast dinner and instead being given a luke warm bowl of thin gruel. You know it is not what you need, but you have no other choice but to eat it and try not to think too much about roast beef and Yorkshire puddings covered in rich onion gravy.

When I lost Violet, I used to go and sit in the church, not because I felt moved religiously, but because she had always taken me there. All I felt was the desperate emptiness, but I just needed some indication or hint of a connection, some proof that I had actually been with her, I just needed something to remain constant. But of course it did not. It was like standing on a thin plank of wood balanced precariously on the surface of quick sand. One wrong move and I would come a cropper, but nothing could really stop that from happening. Even if you don't choose to give in whole-heartedly to the pain and let yourself feel it, it is there waiting for you in the darkness, waiting for the moment when you close your eyes for just a second or turn off the light, and then it will swoop in and grab you by the throat. I found that it was better not to fight that battle. As long as you have a steadying force, a point on the horizon you can keep your eyes on so as not to lose the way back to the living.

Charlotte will need to find a steadying force, an anchor to attach her to the world of the living, for leaving it all that early would just be a waste. For me it was Charlotte and James and Ann who provided my point of reference, my day mark, my light house.

Sixty Six

2nd January 2006

Dear Mum,

I can't quite believe that a year has passed when it only feels like last week.

I am off to some strange Wassailing parade on Borough High Street with my friends.

Love,
XX

Sixty Seven

1st February 2006

Dear Mum,

I wonder who I will become. I have lost my mother, my blessed beloved steadying defining bench-mark and I barely recognise the world anymore.

I am almost desperate to change my reality as it is cold and familiar. I don't seem to recognise my relationships as those I had before. They are different. I am different. I don't think I like it here.

I also wonder if my memory of before is false. Was it not as I remember it? Was our family this painful before? Were we this difficult before? Did I miss something?

Either way I am ready for a change, a rebirth of sorts. But what if I am reborn and all is the same? What if I am the same? What if nothing changes and I wake up and think, "Oh. Is that it?"

I am sitting in a very draughty waiting room, waiting for my train. It is cold, and the wooden seats are very hard on my backside, despite its more recently-found fleshy padding. The lights keep flickering on and off and I am very eager for the train to arrive, but somehow it feels like it is taking too long. I am torn between being bored waiting, and anxious that I have forgotten to pack something really important.

Much love,
XX

Sixty Eight

8th February 2006

Dear Mum,

I wonder how much of me is a product of my family and my ancestry? I am not unique at all, just a carbon copy of my grandmothers, my great-grandmothers, and my mother.

I am still waiting, but I am not sure exactly what I am waiting for. I feel like I need a new life, a new me, a new name in order to carry on here. I feel like I should be re-examining something, but what I don't know. If I were to be reborn into life, what name would I take? Tell me, Mumsie, what would you call me a second time around? What name would you give me?

I would like to shed this skin of fear, angst, jealousy, pain, sorrow, inadequacy. I would like to shed it and step into a lighter life, one where I do not feel like I am being dragged down all the time and dragging others down with me.

Tonight I find myself thinking of the time that my last boyfriend proposed to me in Stratford upon Avon. The parrot in the guesthouse that wolf whistled, and how I thought the proprietor was a bit strange as I didn't know there was a parrot, and all I could hear was someone wolf whistling loudly on the landing all day.

It feels like a different lifetime, and it is as if I am packing away my memories in a trunk, all carefully wrapped in tissue paper and I mustn't forget to add the moth balls in case somebody comes along and nibbles them round the edges, just like the mouse-chewed carpet we discovered the morning we were supposed to give it to Grandma Payton for

Christmas. But I don't want to leave that life behind as you are there and I am afraid I would have to leave you behind.

Perhaps I would like to integrate everything slightly better so that my memories become memories and not hang-ups. That they are things that happened once, but that they chiselled and sanded and shaped me, not that they are me, that there is more to the person I am today than just those events. They are merely facets on the crystal, not covering the whole face of it like a dark cloth.

Much love,
XX

Sixty Nine: Violet

My dearest granddaughter, you already have another name. It was given to you by your grandfather when you were born, all those months after I had left. If you must choose a name to be used only before the gods, then look into your heart and find it there, search within your soul and you will see. Ask for help to find it and your grandfather will step in close to you and with all the energy he can muster he will whisper it in your ear, clearly enunciating every syllable. Violet.

If you asked your friend the psychic she would tell you, or even your own dear sister Ann, who has of late been having what she describes as "conversations" with us. She is not losing her mind as she fears; she is reaching across the divide and finding us there.

Shakespeare may have asked, "What is in a name?" through the heart-sick ponderings of his young heroine Juliet, but some names are destined to be stamped on your soul, and this choice will be one of them. You could travel down through the generations and this name would stay with you.

Some traditions record that God has "secret" names of power known only to those chosen few, those who have earned the right to use them through long study of great dusty old tomes or great feats of magic; Yahweh, Tetragrammaton, Adonai, the ninety nine sacred names of Allah; call on a secret name and you can bend the force of that being to your own will. Call upon the archangels by name and they are compelled to help you.

Remember the story of Rumplestiltskin that you loved so much as a child? Remember the power that was held in his name? The princess was only able to banish him when she learned what his true name was, and once she uttered it once, he knew he could no longer have power over her. The tables had turned, and the power had shifted. Choose your name very carefully my sweet, and be careful who you share it with, for when they learn it, they can command you.

This name Violet to you will have similar connotations. For someone to know this name is the ultimate in trust, but the gods will not leave you so vulnerable; for someone to break that trust will only spell trouble for them later, not through anything you might do, but because your name will be guarded by all who bore the name before you, call on you and they will call on us all.

The name like its sweet-smelling namesake, will herald a new time for you, one of returned happiness and sweetness in life. With this name imprinted on your soul you will learn to live again and you will learn to love life again. And yet, my little flower, it will remind you that in life there is no greater quality than the humility shown by the tiniest and most delicate of little lives, and that there is beauty in the smallest detail just as there is in the wider world. There is beauty in the largest nebula, and in the tiniest snowflake, and the world is contained in them both. As above, so below. So within as without. Artists for generations have tried to inspire the same sense of awe that we have when we look at nature. There is as much beauty in hearing the waves lap against the shore or in Mozart's Clarinet Concerto. The Violet is not trying too hard; it just is. It is small, it is humble and yet it displays the most beautiful purple hue. It is violet light, it is violet perfume, it is violet colour, but it is also the fresh green scent of chlorophyll.

But then of course, I could be biased. It is my name after all.

Seventy

24th March 2006

Dearest Mumsie,

This morning I feel angry with you for abandoning me. So angry I am just steaming inside. Go figure that one out. What a stupid thing to feel.

There is so much going on at the moment, my concentration seems to go like a dragonfly. Dad has now met someone he likes very much, and has moved to Guernsey as he got fed up commuting over there all the time. It feels like a very small way of mentioning such a big change, but it is his life and I am happy he has found something to live for. Of course that leaves the house empty at the moment, which brings with it a completely different set of feelings.

It is Mother's Day this weekend, and it really hurts. This year Ann and I are both trying to think "Happy Mother's Day, Mumsie" every time we hear or see anything instead of last year when it felt like I was being slapped around the face hard every time I went into a shop and saw all the displays decked out in blue and pink and yellow, all the colours of spring that you loved so much.

I bought a jasmine plant for you and put it in the window in the hallway so that I see it each time I leave the house, or return. I still miss you so much, but somehow it feels a bit less obsessive than it did last year, and yet it is unrelenting nonetheless. Sometimes I would get a sense of you or a faint smell of your perfume on the breeze, but I haven't smelled or felt you around in months. It is as if my sense of you is muffled, which really makes me look at your loss in a more absolute way. There is no denying it, no cushion, no baffling. Just cold hard steel.

I wonder where you are and what you are doing, but this lack of you makes me question everything. What if we have got it all wrong, and when we die we just stop? What if there is no other, no after? And I know that the reason we don't know is the whole point, because if we knew there was an after, we wouldn't bother doing anything here; we would just have no reason to. Which is one of my frustrations with organised religion, don't worry that your life is utter shite, because it is supposed to be. When you die you will go to heaven and get your rewards. Although part of me thinks heaven of sorts is still there. Am I just hedging my bets? Who knows?

What do you think Mumsie?

Love,
XX

Seventy One: Margaret

What do I think? That is an interesting idea. It could be right, that when our bodies die we must stop, although if that is the case someone obviously forgot to tell me that was what I was supposed to do. Maybe we are all part of an elaborate hoax. Maybe we all live as part of a giant hologram and the physical life is just an illusion. Perhaps one morning we will all wake up, just like the Jefferson Airplane song says, to find a hookah smoking caterpillar has given you the call, and one pill makes you larger and one makes you small. Or maybe you have to choose between the blue pill and the red pill in order to see the matrix for what it really is, a place where physics has it all wrong, and time and space do not really exist at all. Go ask Alice; perhaps she will have an answer for you.

Or alternatively, you could just take every opportunity that life and death give you, and decide to embrace them with both hands, and all the thinking be damned. Don't get me wrong, thinking is imperative to avoid a life lived in a half-light, but not when it is at the expense of your self-worth or sanity, not when it disables you completely and leaves you stuck in procrastination and stagnation.

My lovely, I would advise you (and I think you can hear me even if you think you can't) that just for a while you should stop thinking and start living. Stop picking at the scabs and start experiencing pure, wild, abandoned, energetic, experiential, magical, eighty-seven percent cocoa solids life.

And then afterwards, when you have got into your little boat and journeyed into the West where all things go to die, and I await you patiently on the other shore, I will sit you down in front of the fire and, steaming mugs of tea in hand we will mull over what it all means.

But just for now, just for me, just keep putting one foot in front of the other. Soon you will start to experience little moments of joy to punctuate the darkness, and then little by little, the light spells will come more frequently, until one day you will suddenly realise that you are living life again, and how did that happen? But all along, through all of it, we your ancestors will walk alongside you. I will be with you always.

And when you eventually come to find me, I will show you the truth of what is here, what we are, and what is there where you are. To tell you now would spoil the surprise, and while you are limited to what you think the human brain can understand, it would not make sense. The truth is beyond human language and beyond human thought.

Seventy Two: Charlotte

It is the appointed time. I tap on the glass like Kathy wanting to come in from the cold. A cloaked figure both familiar and mysterious opens the door and asks if I wish to proceed. I nod and croak "Yes." I am given admittance.

The door is closed behind us, and I am led though the dark inside and down the narrow staircase, where a seat awaits me in a room lit only by flickering candle light. Soft music plays in the background, lulling me into a momentary state of relaxation until the figure returns and asks me again if I would like to proceed. Again I nod and say yes.

The figure bids me to remove the trappings of the outside world and be seated, and I am left alone again, wondering what will happen and wondering if I am mad to do this. I decide I must trust the process; for even the worst that could happen cannot be worse than where I have been living. I wrap myself in a cloak that has been left for me on the chair, and start to gaze into the flickering candle flame. Time passes. An hour. Maybe two. I have no way of telling.

The figure returns again and reads me the words of the journey I must go on. This is the six of swords, the journey across water, a rite of passage.

Now it is autumn and the falling fruit
And the long journey towards oblivion.
Build then the ship of death, for you must take
The longest journey, to oblivion.[2]

I welcome it, whole-heartedly. If this is what it takes to leave this scarred and battered self behind, I welcome it with open arms. May the dark lord Osiris come for me now; I am ready.

And die the death, the long and painful death
That lies between the old self and the new.
Already our bodies are fallen, bruised, badly bruised,
Already our souls are oozing through the exit of the cruel
bruise.
Already the dark and endless ocean of the end
Is washing through the breachers of our wounds,
Already the flood is upon us.

I hold my breath and try to steady my nerves. This is what I have waited for. This is what I have worked for. All of my life converges in on this moment in time, this place, this night. At last I can rid myself of her.

Oh build your ship of death, your little ark
And furnish it with food, with little cakes and wine

For the dark flight down oblivion.
Piecemeal the body dies, and the timid soul
Has her footing washed away, as the dark flood rises.

I lose my footing and allow her to tumble into the darkness, willing her to be gone. She has served me well and long, but now she must leave me in order that I can go on. If I am ever to find my Mother again, she must leave me.

We are dying, we are dying, we are all of us dying
And nothing will stay the death-flood rising within us
And soon it will rise on the world, the outside world.

We are dying, we are dying, piecemeal our bodies are
dying and our strength leaves us,
And our souls cower naked in the dark rain over the flood,
Cowering in the last branches of the tree of our life.

We are dying, we are dying, so all we can do
Is now be willing to die, and to build the ship

Of death to carry the soul on the longest journey.

As I get into the little boat, darkness falls around me. I am blind now, helpless, and naked as the day I was born. There are no lies left, no masks, and nothing is hidden. Now there is only my cold, naked soul. I pray I am worthy. I pray I am worthy to stand before my gods and swear an oath to them.

Now launch the small ship, now as the body dies
and life departs, launch out, the fragile soul
in the fragile ship of courage, the ark of faith
with its store of food and little cooking pans
and change of clothes,
upon the flood's black waste
upon the waters of the end
upon the sea of death, where still we sail
darkly for we cannot steer, and have no port.

The boat seems to drift along of its own accord, steered by a current that I can't quite feel, but while all I can see is the darkness all around, I can still hear the gentle slapping of the water against the hull of the boat.

There is no port, there is nowhere to go
Only the deepening blackness darkening still
Blacker upon the soundless, ungurgling flood
Darkness at one with darkness, up and down
And sideways utterly dark, so there is no direction
anymore
She is not seen, for there is nothing to see her by.
She is gone! Gone! And yet
Somewhere she is there.
Nowhere!

At last the boat scrapes upon the shore, and I can feel the sand and gravel beneath the hull bringing the boat to a complete standstill. I cautiously listen for sounds around me.

A rush of anxiety washes through me, but I feel for the sides of the boat and get to my feet, hesitatingly, and set by step feel my way out of the boat. The gravel and cold water feel harsh against the soles of my feet, and my skin begins to feel painful momentarily, but as I make my way further up the beach, the gravel gives way to sand and gradually I cease to feel where my feet were, it is as if my body has left me.

And everything is gone, the body is gone
Completely under, gone, entirely gone.
The upper darkness is heavy as the lower,
between them the little ship
is gone

It is the end, it is oblivion.

Far away I hear voices start to chant; the sound starts slowly but then begins to pick up speed and the voices gradually get louder and louder. I try to pick out how many voices there are, but in the darkness and without the blessing of sight to help make sense of the new world around me it is impossible to tell. Things so simple in daylight are not simple now. I can assume nothing. I can pick out some of the words in the chant but they make little sense to me, but then the language shifts and it is no longer recognisable. My breath has started to match the beat of their voices, and my heart is thumping against my rib cage.

And yet I begin to sense I can feel someone next to me, their hand on my shoulder steadying my nerves, I can hear them breathing softly although I intuit they do not need to breathe for physical reasons. I catch a faint whiff of a familiar perfume, and the smell anchors me into a state of calm, of being held and of being nurtured.

And yet out of eternity a thread
Separates itself on the blackness,
A horizontal thread

174

That fumes a little with pallor upon the dark

The voices far away dissolve into what sounds like laughter, and despite my unusual predicament I find myself smiling. Then a rush of cold air signals to me that a door has opened, and someone steps in close to me. He is Hermes, the messenger of the gods, and he reassures me with a flourish of chivalry. He has come swift-footed to guide me the rest of the way. Finally he whispers, "Your name?" The question hangs in the air for a split second before I speak, uncertain, testing, but I know now it is right.

"Violet," I say. "My name is Violet."

Is it illusion or does the pallor fume
a little higher?
Ah wait, wait, for there's the dawn,
The cruel dawn of coming back to life
Out of oblivion

I get to my feet and allow myself to be led by my quicksilver friend, into a room which is warmed by the light of many candles, where I am awaited by those gentle souls who will take me away from my world of pure pain to a world of balance, a world where life can be lived again. But this will not be without its trials. I come to a stop at the gateway and a deep voice challenges me.

I take a breath to steady myself and, voice haltering, I speak the words I was given. Something in the atmosphere changes, a breath that was held is let go, and I am welcomed in.

The flood subsides, and the body, like a worn sea-shell
Emerges strange and lovely.
And the little ship wings home, faltering and lapsing
On the pink flood.

Finally, I speak the words that will be imprinted upon my unconscious mind for all eternity. A token has been taken lest I should weaken; my life is now given to my gods, willingly and with a full sense of what that might mean. It is no longer mine to squander. It is no longer mine to be surrendered in a pool of tablets and alcohol, even if I wanted it to be. By their bidding I must live it to its fullness.

At last the sun breaks through the cloud cover, just enough to remind me that it is there. I am anointed and blessed and presented to the guardians.

And the frail soul steps out, into her house again
Filling the heart with peace.
Swings the heart renewed with peace
Even of oblivion

Bonds are removed and my sight is restored. I look upon the faces around me, reassuring me, looking with love. I have found a new home.

Oh build your ship of death, oh build it!
For you will need it.
For the voyage of oblivion awaits you.

My name is Violet. I was born on the 3rd June at approximately 10.30 pm, eighteen months after my beloved Mother passed away. Loving hands coaxed me into my new life, whilst loving voices whispered and chanted words of encouragement. Afterwards we feasted together, and then in the early hours of the morning, I made my way home to my little flat and the warmth and safety of my bed.

Seventy Three

20th June 2006

Dear Mumsie,

I am not sure if this new suit of clothes fits me that well yet. I feel a little uncomfortable with it. I have actually changed my life, my values, my lifestyle, and finally my religion. I am not sure if I was expecting fireworks, or to be able to shape-shift or something. I haven't got that ability, but I do feel different, and yet if you asked me to define how, I wouldn't quite be able to put my finger on it.

I seem to spend a lot of time feeling really tired, which I think means I am still doing a lot of processing at night. Last night I dreamed strange dreams of someone holding me close and telling me how it will be, but when someone in the dream asked me what had been said, all I could say was "I have no recollection of that. I cannot remember. I must have been touched by God himself."

Life is eerily confusing at the moment.

Love,
XX

Seventy Four: Margaret

My Lovey,

I had the most wonderful experience last night that I must
tell you about. I say "last night" and yet time here doesn't
mean the same as it does where you are, but just as the sun
was setting and I was sitting in my garden beneath the
mountain ash tree having a lively discussion with some
interesting souls I have met here, one of them suddenly
looked over my shoulder and pointed to something behind
me.

My dearest Charlotte, I turned to see what was there, and
imagine my surprise when there, standing next to the
blossoming jasmine, was you!

You were shimmering softly in the pale glow of evening
light, and the edges of you were slightly blurred, as if you
were merging into the midsummer night itself. You looked at
me, and smiled, and then a moment later you were gone,
leaving only the empty space behind you.

"Have you any idea what this means?" my companions
asked. I shook my head.

"She is learning to travel between the worlds. With time
and practice she may get steadier and stronger," my
companion continued, "but she will need to practice."

"Will we be able to speak to each other?" I asked.

"Eventually," he said. "Although it is difficult to guess for
how long she will be able to sustain her visits."

He explained to me that since we all come from the place
where I am now, sometimes a soul can get homesick and
while your physical body is sleeping, you soul can take flight
and travel wherever it most desires. Some people travel the
globe and visit far off places they have always wanted to visit
but never had the opportunity, and some come here to visit

loved ones or to consult with the wise ones that guide them. Sadly, for the sake of maintaining the order of things, mostly when you awake you may remember little of your night-time adventures, other than a vague sense of having been busy and feeling tired as a result.

But, lovey, just ponder what this means! How exciting, that you and I will not have to wait all your lifetime in order to see and recognise each other again. I know I can come and see you in the blink of an eye, but now you can see me too! Apparently it takes practice, a lot of practice, and you may need some help.

Perhaps you should go and see your friend the psychic again? I am sure she would know someone who could teach you. My love, there is a whole world of possibilities, and the adventures are just beginning!

Much love,

Mum
XX

Seventy Five

19th July 2006

Dear Mum,

It is one of those hot sticky nights when you wake up with whatever little you are wearing stuck to your body like a second skin. I can't remember what cold feels like. I mean, I literally can't remember or imagine what it feels like to be in a cool temperature or to be in winter.

I have woken again at four in the morning, and my mind is racing and I can't get back to sleep. The air feels as if a storm is about to break, with that heavy stillness that weighs down on the earth and allows no free movement.

I have awoken with a strange sense that I have been somewhere else. I feel drained as if I have been busy somewhere, and yet, if you were to ask me where I thought I had been and what I thought I had been doing, I would have no focussed idea of where or what. And I keep getting a faint scent of jasmine, although I know there is none in the flat.

This life feels so different, and when I look into the future now I see possibility, instead of the darkness, I see a vague shimmering hope instead of the intensity of thick tar that covered my future before. I am not sure where this path may take me, but at least now I feel a sense of resolve that if I have another thirty years or so here without you, I had better make the most of it and come back with some interesting stories instead of squandering it on feeling bad.

Perhaps adventures are the way forward? Perhaps living life to the full is the new black? I don't know, what do you think Mumsie?

I think I have a lot of new things to learn, and I hope you will be able to join me for at least some of it, even if I can't see you there. I would like to learn ways in which I could sense you there at least.

Perhaps I should look into having my friend teach me ways of plugging in? She teaches Psychic Development classes in South Kensington. I wonder if that would help? The only thing is, I wonder if I should wait a while? I don't want to be obsessive about contacting you. I remember you mentioning one of your lame ducks who lost her father, and then spent the rest of the time attending Spiritualist Churches at every opportunity hoping for messages from him. I don't think that would be helpful for either of us. It might even be disruptive as well as imagine trying to get something done when the phone keeps ringing every five minutes, and you can't give it your full attention because you have to keep getting up to answer the phone and speak to whoever it is that needs something on the other end.

I don't want to be another one of your lame ducks, Mumsie. I don't want to interfere and disturb you in whatever it is you are doing over there.

Missing you Mum,
XX

Seventy Six

13th August 2007

Dear Mum,

Well, I have been going to the Psychic Development classes. I managed to persuade two of my friends to come with me, but I am not sure if they are getting as much out of it as I am.

It is strange, as we started with Psychometry and I was really bad at it. It is the process where you hold an object and get information from it. We started with a session of "bum psychometry" where you sit on someone's chair and see what you can get, but Mum, I swear to god I got nothing. Nada. It was so humiliating. But then slowly, each session I found I got a little bit more. At the end of the course, I was fully expecting to tell my teacher I wouldn't be continuing, and yet when I went to the next session, we were doing readings and of course mine said I needed to carry on. So here we are. Psychic School is continuing, even though I thought I was psychically constipated!

For the last few weeks, I have been trying to concentrate on your life, and not so much on your death. We had so many happy times together, and your life was filled with so much good and so many varied expressions and experiences, it seems unfair of me to only concentrate on how you died, of how you were in death, how your face looked so smooth and soft and line free, and how empty of you you looked.

Please help me to remember.

Your loving daughter,
XX

Seventy Seven: Margaret

Dear Charlotte,

Where should I begin? I will begin with you and I perched on a rock on a hillside overlooking the sea in Cornwall in the Scilly Isles. Remember that day we sat and talked of how this wilderness, this nature, this landscape was your culture? Your father climbed down to the rocks to see the water rush in at Piper's Hole, and we sat above, chilled by the wind, but safe from the waves that smashed against the rocks and flung their white spray high into the air before splattering down onto the rocks again from above. We sat and felt the sonic boom as the water crashed against the rocks beneath us, and as the moon rose high in the evening sky, we walked back across the top of the island to the cottage with the wood-fire where your sister and her partner were, and then all shared in the cottage pie that had been warming in the oven.

I loved spending that time with you. I loved our conversations, and the fun we had. And I was proud to think you were my daughter. Whatever I had done in life, whatever my faults and mistakes, I had you and your brother and your sister, which meant I must have done something right.

Your loving,

Mum
XX

Seventy Eight

29th August 2007

Dear Mum,

I have just had a magical few days at home. Why is it, that wherever I live in the world, wherever I travel or work, Dartmoor will always be home? It is as if wherever I go my soul will always be there.

The night before I travelled down, Dad came to stay, which was lovely, as he was in London on a training course for the voluntary work he is doing in the Channel Islands.

The house feels very different now that it is empty, but I am at least grateful it is still there. I would be absolutely heartbroken if anything ever happened to it. I would so love to go home and live there now, but the challenge will always be in how to earn a living there. Ironic really that I spent the later years of my adolescence longing to leave, and now I long to go home.

Anyway, Ann, Mary, Raven and I came to the music Festival that our lovely neighbours were having, and Raven and I took some of our crafts down to sell. We had a great time, and there was a lot to see. The music was fun – my favourite bits were really seeing our lovely friends playing their music. It was stunning. They are both so talented it quite blew me away. I was watching them thinking, "Those are my friends up there!"

It also gave us the opportunity to really explore the land and see what they have done with it down there. There were shrines all over, and different gardens, and a little dipping pool that they have shaped in the stream. I found such a sense of peace down there.

After the festival finished, we stayed down there for the rest of the week, but we all felt a bit unwell. I was really craving some quiet time, and seeing the house empty of you still feels strange, so it all felt very raw.

One day I snuck off to Happy Valley on my own, because I really needed to have a howl. When I had howled and quietened down, it felt like I needed to shift the energy a bit and really "cleanse" myself, so I stripped off and jumped into the Wallabrook, right beneath my favourite willow tree, where there is a little natural dipping pool. I completely submerged myself in the ice cold water; head, naked body and all. The shock of the cold water was certainly enough to give me the energy shift I was looking for, as it is very difficult to stop from giving a yell as your head goes under.

The one at the farm is under a willow tree too – I wonder if it is a coincidence or if the root growth encourages the brook to form in that way? I love the fact that Happy Valley is still a place that you can be running around in just your skin in full daylight and not see a soul. I am realising how important that sense of solitude was to me growing up, and how much I miss that in London.

I am not sure that this has been the most relaxing holiday I felt I needed, but at least I have had time to re-connect a little. I haven't even made it up to the cemetery yet, but this feels almost immaterial as I know you are not there. I think you are more likely to be dancing sky clad with me by the Wallabrook than in the quiet, calm of the graveyard.

XX

Seventy Nine

8th September 2007

Dear Mum,

Dad's wedding is approaching at a speed of knots, and I feel quite disconcerted. I have finally booked the flight.

I have been doing the Denise Linn "Soul Coaching" programme this week. I am clearing clutter like you wouldn't believe, cleaning like a wild cleaning thing. I have booked the NLP course for November, and yesterday I stayed home to work on the pre-course study, but ended up cleaning the flat from top to bottom first. The general idea is that if you clear out the space around you, you give yourself space to breathe and think clearly, the ideas come through from your soul more easily, and I have to say, it certainly works for me.

I have been thinking more and more about going back to acting. I miss that creative process, and I miss the joy I used to feel when I was acting. Instead of feeling bitter about it like I did when I took a step back from it before, I feel a bit more positive, and this week it struck me like a thunderbolt, if I had the money, I would apply for a Post graduate course at one of the big five drama schools, so that this time I would have the solid foundation I didn't have last time. If I had the money, I would do it differently this time. My heart's desire hasn't gone away, I had just repressed it. But how will I find the money? How will I make it happen? Or should I just shut up and write?

I feel confused, but at least I feel as if I have got my fire back a bit.

Love,
XX

Eighty

13th September 2007

Dear Mum,

I so desperately wish I could go back to the Scillies, but somehow I just can't bring myself to. I tried to last year, and it just felt so hard without you, so impossibly bleak and empty, and so lacking in love and life. But to think of never going back just seems so desperately sad.

Whenever I go home to the house now, I walk through the rooms you once lived in; I touch the things that were yours and I read the books that were yours, I listen to the music that was yours and it tears a hole in my soul and my heart all over again, knowing that you are not coming back there.

But somehow going back to the island seems harder; as if it is one step too far and I can only spread myself so thin. I think it has to be the house that I concentrate my efforts on, but then I must lose the island. Our island. The place that we spent so many happy holidays together since I was small.

I feel bereft of you all over again.

XX

Eighty One: Margaret

Charlotte,

I am with you wherever you go. For now you must accept that some things are too hard, and you are human. You can only do so much, and it is still early days yet.

I want you to be happy so much. In fact I will go a step further and tell you that you need to be happy.

When you grieve and feel the sadness of the loss of me, your energy becomes dense and heavy. If you can see beyond and start to do the things that inspire you, you will lift up and connect with me far more easily. Charlotte, there will come a time when you will be able to feel when I am with you, there will come a time when you can sense us there with you, and distinguish between us. You will see that it doesn't matter where in the world you are, as long as you are happy and connecting with the energy that inspires you.

You could stand on the surface of the moon and feel us with you, if that was a place that inspired you. The island is a truly special place, and one day you will go back there. Maybe you will go back with my grand children and show them all the places that we shared together, and tell them stories about Grandma so that they can sense me too.

This physical life is so fleeting, it will pass like a rush of wind through a valley, and I want you to treasure your experiences while you can and then when you cross the veil to join me here, we will walk upon the island again. We will walk across its white sandy beaches and dip our toes into the icy clear waters, and listen to the oyster catchers in the bay.

Your loving,

Mum

Eighty Two

Dear Mum,

It is Ann's fortieth birthday today, and two days after Dad's wedding. It has been quite a rollercoaster of a weekend. I have cried, howled, laughed, and been excited, nervous, angry, happy...

The hotel we all stayed in was lovely. I had a really nice room that opened out onto a roof terrace. It was the same hotel that Ann and Mary stayed in, as well as Aunty Jane and Uncle Lawrence, cousin Jenny, your special friend Ruth and her husband Richard, Steve and Lucy from next door, and even your other friends from the Soroptimists were there. We got to see loads of Ruth and Richard, and dragged Steve and Lucy round with us all weekend, so it was lovely.

Of course the weekend was not without its dramas, and rumblings and arguments. It is strange because I am sure when you were around we just didn't have that level of disagreements and fights. I wonder if I am imagining that or if your presence just managed to diffuse most things? Or maybe I was just blind to it all then? I don't think it is my imagination, because my teacher in my spiritual family also has that ability to make politicking and conflicts go completely under the radar.

Anyway, the wedding was lovely and very tasteful. The world has indeed changed completely now, which feels very strange, but I am glad that Dad is happy and has found a purpose again. Forgive me if I don't write all of the details of the whole thing to you, but I don't feel I want or need to. If you were there you would have seen it, but somehow Dad's life after you doesn't feel like my story to comment on.

Love,
XX

Eighty Three

15th October 2007

Dear Mum,

I have woken up with five o'clock in the morning brain race, just on a day when I will need to have my wits about me as I have Psychic School followed by a class at the bookshop.

So what has woken me up? Work is progressing well on the NLP pre-study – I only have a few weeks to go now. I had some new headshots done a few weeks ago by Phoenix, and I am not quite sure why, and I am trying not to get into "but when?" thought patterns, as trying to push things too quickly invariably leads to problems.

So here is the thing. I desperately want to do NLP Coaching, as well as a coaching programme in California, and also a two year MA at the Drama Centre, and the NLP Master Practitioner programme. There is not one I want to do more or less than the others, and I am awake and stressing about all of them, and yet I would need muchos mullah to do any of them, let alone all of them, which of course I don't have.

I keep thinking of the old family friend who had been so nasty to us all when you died, as they had felt entitled to come and see you, even though you had said you didn't want visitors and they had not wanted to see you when you were well and were standing outside their house trying to reach out to them. I remember how they sent a letter to you saying how mean Dad was, and how cruel we had all been to them, and how the letter arrived in a birthday card to you that arrived the day after you died. I stand by our decision to honour your wish to not have people parade through your bedroom, looking for absolution or farewell. It is painful to think of, and I don't know why it has come up now. People behave so strangely sometimes.

Love,
XX

Eighty Four

1st November 2007

Dear Mum,

I have just come back from the most amazing weekend away with my spiritual family. We caught the train to Bristol for the weekend to meet up with some lovely people, and it was quite exquisite. We had guests over from America too, so all in all it was one of those deeply enriching times that I know I am so lucky to have access to.

We went out to Stanton Drew on Saturday to visit with a local druid circle who were holding a ritual at the stone circle, and we were treated like honoured guests. Then we went back to our base and held our own little Halloween party on Saturday evening, just for family and honoured guests.

After dinner the conversation turned to future plans. I have been yearning so hard for my acting days recently, that I mentioned this over dinner. Strangely, one of my friends nearly choked on his houmous, and said,

"Drama school? I don't think so! What about a baby?"

Of course that was my cue to choke on my houmous.

Apparently my friend is very good at picking up signs of possible pregnancy on the ether, and he said he has been picking this up around me for some time.

But who am I going to have children with? Stephen always swore blind he wouldn't have children.

And what about drama school?

As I write this I have a little voice in my head saying,

"You know your life doesn't end when you have children."

Is that you Mum?

Love,
XX

Eighty Five

29th October 2007

Dear Mum,

Well, Psychic School classes are continuing apace, and I feel as if my inner life is one of great expansion at the moment. I am learning so many things, I am blessed. The friends who started Psychic School with me in the beginning dropped out after a while and I continued alone, but it felt fine. I feel this path is one I have to walk alone to a certain extent. (The cynical voice of Stephen echoes in my head telling me we are born alone and we die alone, but then you didn't die alone did you, Mumsie? Or not completely alone anyway.)

The NLP Practitioner course is now a short hop away, and it is the same one that Ann and Mary studied, so I am really excited.

Yay! How learning makes me feel alive again!

Love,
XX

Eighty Six

5th November 2007

Dear Mum,

I have just completed day three of my NLP training, and I can't work out if we are part of some mass hysteria or if it is just magic! It is truly ingenious, and I love it!

The trainer started by telling us to say goodbye to our lives, as by the end of the week, the life we will be going back to will be completely different from the one we left on the first morning. This didn't scare me, as if anything I was desperate to leave the old life behind, as it is so painful. I am embracing these changes, as I don't feel as if I have anything to lose. The old life doesn't serve anymore, so let it go, degree by degree.

The basic premise of NLP (if you condense it down to its most simple components) is that we have a conscious mind that does all our thinking for us (the captain of the boat) and an unconscious mind that takes care of our body, our feelings and everything else (the crew of the boat). The magical part is the unconscious mind, but the difficulty is in getting instructions to it, as it doesn't speak language, it speaks in symbols and the aim of NLP is to get the two minds working together in rapport, so that your conscious mind gives the orders and your unconscious mind knows what you want it to do.

Most of the time they don't work in rapport and that is when we run into difficulties. NLP is a bit like the secret manual of instructions for your brain that the manufacturer forgot to give you when you bought it. It is so simple, and yet exquisitely effective.

I feel like I may be on to something. I think that just like Dad deciding last year that he wanted to meet someone new, I have been searching for something that would inspire me again. I think that all of the things that I have been studying this year have been it. I think that inspiration is the key that makes us all want to live, because life isn't life if you simply exist to get from birth to death in as few difficult steps as possible.

I want to love my time here, and not resent it. That way when I do get to come home and find you (for I am not sure that I will ever be at home here again without you) I will have something I have learned to share with you.

I don't want to be dry and brittle like the dead plants.

Love,
XX

Eighty Seven: Margaret

Learning new things is such a luxury in life, and was one of the highlights of my time there. I always loved learning new skills, probably because I finished school earlier than I would have liked and always felt as if I had missed out on the experience of going to university or college. Whenever I went on courses later in life, I always felt really privileged. Learning does something fundamental on the inside. It is not just that you are learning about external things, but that you are growing and evolving and learning more about yourself too. I loved that process of change and development, as I was always curious to see where I ended up next.

When Charlotte was about seventeen, I finally got my wish and went to University as a mature student. I spent two years studying for a real live proper qualification, and I was so proud of myself when I finished. The day of my graduation was one of the highlights of my life for me; it was one of the few things I did allow myself to bask in the glory of, for just a little while, before it was time to get back to work and use it for the benefit of someone other than myself. I kept the certificate framed on the wall, but rather than have it somewhere prominent, I put it on the wall in the utility room, right beside the ironing board, just to remind me that while certificates might be well and good, there is still work to do in the world, and we all still to roll up our sleeves and get on with the business of helping those that we can help.

When I was a young maid, I had wanted to be a nurse, but at the time my Father persuaded me that would not be a nice job to have, as there is all that mess of bodily fluids and cleaning up to do, but the essence of nursing that appealed to me was in the ability to help people and to make a difference in their lives. I learned as I got older that this was possible to do, without having to wear a pair of gloves and an apron. It is not just their physical health that needs looking after, and often physical symptoms are indicative of something going on in the inside. When I later worked in a drop in centre for street drinkers and the homeless, I realised that people didn't really care what your qualifications were, all they really needed was someone to listen to them once in a while, and for someone to seem like they cared. But don't let that fool you; it is not all bleeding hearts and dabbing their tears with a hanky. Sometimes they needed a swift kick up the bottom as much as they needed the sympathy.

The truth is we all have choices in life, no matter how much we fool ourselves that we may have been a victim of chance, or fate. We all make choices every second of our lives, whether it is what colour underwear to put on, or whether or not to be nice to the stranger standing in front of us, whether to share the bad mood we are in, or whether to share a smile and a kind word. We can choose to punish the world for the harsh things it has done to us and be a victim, or we can choose to take responsibility for our own behaviour and just get on with it.

Anyone who tries to tell you otherwise is just kidding themselves, and making life much harder for themselves. When you can't change the whole world, there is nothing that says you can't change the little corner of it which is yours. Sometimes the kindest thing you can do for someone is to point out they are not being honest with themselves if they think that life is out of their control. There is always another choice. There is always another way. Free will is the greatest gift that was ever given to human beings, but sometimes we get so caught up with all the unnecessary excuses, that we forget to look in the mirror and see that the creator of our own universe is the person staring right back at us.

Eighty Eight

9th November 2007

Dear Mum,

Well, I am now a qualified Practitioner of NLP and hypnosis. How weird is that?

I feel like I have been completely transformed this week, and yet I suspect I will not fully realise just how much for a while yet.

As the training involved studying the interventions and then practicing them on each other, I feel as if my brain has had a complete re-install. I have re-installed the operating system and it feels very... well, clean.

I spent virtually the whole week in a hypnotic state as well, so although I felt really nervous on day one and was expecting the first few days to feel really uncomfortable, an hour or so in to our first morning I realised with surprise that I felt really relaxed. It was about three days later when I realised that this was because our teacher had put us all n a light hypnotic state in the first few minutes of the course when he gave his opening talk, so it was really relaxing and the other forty or so people on the training were absolutely lovely. All of that meant that the learning was much easier to do, and even the harder bits were easier to deal with.

Several times a day I would have a "eureka" moment as something I was learning related to something I have been learning in my other studies. Now, back to Psychic school and the regular programme of studies to see where they all cross over into each other.

Love,
XX

Eighty Nine

26th November 2007

Dear Mum,

I am hereby banishing the bad mood that has enveloped me for the last few weeks. Since Dad's birthday I have felt like pants; really gloomy and depressed, lacking in energy and motivation.

It was only when I started talking to Ann on Sunday that I realised it was because three years ago, around the time of Dad's birthday, you found out you had cancer.

I miss you so much, and I feel like I can't seem to find you no matter what I do. No psychic Development course, no Halloween ritual, no NLP intervention ever seems to bring me to you. I feel so spiritually disconnected from everything at the moment. And I am so homesick too.

I long to reconnect again, to plug into the mains again, but I don't seem to be able to. It is like I am wearing mittens and ear mufflers, and dark glasses in a dark room. And I am sure everyone is standing right behind my shoulders shouting,

"Charlotte! Wake the fuck up!"

But somehow I just can't seem to hear.

I want to feel the magic again, but when I feel like this it is hard to find faith that anything will work. I have no faith in myself or in my abilities.

Love,
XX

Ninety

28th November 2007

Dear Mum,

I have just been to my Psychic School teacher's book launch, and who should arrive like the Grail King in a storm but Phoenix, clutching as usual his favourite deck of cards.

Phoenix, Raven and I snuck off with the tarot deck and while the main focus was for him to read for Raven, in a simple four card throwaway spread he also managed to reassure me, quite a lot.

The upshot of what he read was that I need to go with the flow, that it is bound to feel strange at the moment, as I have stepped out of who I was but have not quite stepped into who I will be. That I shouldn't rush to find the next "project" but just enjoy the scenery for a while.

But the strange thing is he also said there is a young man coming into my life that will be immensely creative and sweep me off my feet. How can that be? What about Stephen?

I feel so immensely privileged to have all these amazing people in my life. I feel as if I am amongst the movers and shakers, that I am right where the action is.

May I be worthy of the company I keep.

Love,
XX

Ninety One

9th December 2007

Dear Mum,

It is the NLP Coaching weekend, and I am en route to Chiswick for day two. This is the bolt on course to the Practitioner certificate. It is really lovely studying this with Ann and Mary, and wow! What an experience!

I went along thinking that after the amazing experience of the Practitioner training we couldn't possibly experience something as life-changing as that when it is only two days long.

How wrong was I?!

The first exercise we did was "Discover Your Own Life Purpose" and my mind was consequently blown by 11.30 in the morning. Everything suddenly makes sense now. My purpose is to experience life to the fullest, experience by sensory exploration, adventures, being creative and interacting with people.

I thought it would be something more complex than that, but now acting, writing and the crafts makes sense to me, so much so it feels like child's play.

My life's purpose isn't to be a famous and successful actor, because my life's purpose is not limited to what job I do, it is bigger than that, and yet somehow far simpler.

I came here for the purpose of really living and being as creative as I can be.

Our teacher says that when your goals and actions are in line with your life's purpose and your values, things come easily and without effort, and you feel happy. It is as simple as testing how you feel at any one given moment, to see if you are on the right track or not, and if there is a negative kinaesthetic feeling, chances are you are in conflict with your values or purpose.

I think the problems I have had with acting and writing so far were that I got sidetracked with the irrelevant bits, as I was trying too hard, and of course I know now that "to try" is a false verb, it pre-supposes failure. Either you can do it, or you can try and then fail. I was chasing the agent, and the idea that I wanted to be paid something for my work, and wasn't remembering the simple joy of creating, and that is not connected to money or the politics of the industry. There was too much stuff getting in the way and it was clouding my connection and making it be a joyless thing, which then takes away the ability to create.

Now I know my life's purpose and my values associated with it, I can learn to reframe things in line with it, then I might have a slightly easier time.

All the time I was worrying about being on the wrong path and I was on the right path all along. But it was the act of worrying about being on the wrong path that was blocking me and stopping me seeing the simple truth, which is so much simpler than I thought it would ever be.

"Daft maid," I can hear you saying in my head.

Love,
XX

Ninety Two: Margaret

When Charlotte was a little girl, she was really imaginative. I don't know what it was, whether it was something in our genes, or something in the water where we lived, but she was always constructing different worlds, largely as a result of the books she read, and she read many, many books. She made her way voraciously through everything she could find, and if it wasn't reading, it was old 1950's films that she used to watch on a tiny black and white TV that we put in her bedroom. And she also loved Marilyn Monroe, a lot. One entire wall in her room was plastered with photos of Marilyn Monroe, the other with Unicorns. I remember being woken up one morning to the sounds of her singing away at the top of her lungs to "Diamonds Are a Girl's Best Friend," which under certain circumstances might be worrying from a thirteen year old, but with Charlotte it was just part of this strange world of contradictions she chose to inhabit. Her father always used to tell her she should marry a millionaire with a cough, but I never thought that would be quite her style. The world she lived in as a teenager may have been a world away from the one I inhabited with young offenders and the wives of prison inmates, but after a while, the two worlds somehow blended and created this girl with imagination and a heart. When she left school at the end of each day, she would come and meet me at the young person's bail hostel I worked in, and when she decided that she wanted to be an actress, I sent her off to work with a colleague of mine who ran a theatre company for young people who needed some help in finding their way. I sometimes thought she was an unusual child; she got on well with the middle class girls in her school, but just as well with the troubled young people in the theatre group, which meant that wherever she may end up in life, I always hoped she would always carry a dose of compassion with her. I suppose it is one of the uncertainties of having children; you can bring them up and teach them your values, but you can't dictate who they will become. They have free will, and they have to make their own choices. All I could hope was that I would give them the tools they needed in order to become good adults who I could be proud of, and they did.

I can remember, years later when I met up with her in London one day, we sat in a coffee shop on Tottenham Court Road, enjoying a day out together, and talked about her life as an actor, and how difficult it was. She was finding it really hard to get paid work, or even to be treated reasonably by the people she was working with. She had spent job after job in dusty, cold uncomfortable places, for little or no money, and she was wondering what she could do differently to find better work, and if there was something she was doing wrong. It was as if she thought there was a secret code that she needed to learn, or a mysterious rule book that everyone else has but she hadn't seen. As we drank our coffee, I very gently said to her that maybe, just maybe, this wasn't the right world for her to inhabit. I asked her if she had ever thought of doing something else instead, something where she would be appreciated, and treated a little better. I knew she was such a sensitive soul, and to live in a world where you would be judged by your outward appearance and so quickly, seemed like a hard place for her to choose to live, and so at odds with everything else we knew.

I think at the time, this question made her think that her whole world was about to come crashing down around her, I could see it on her face; that crumbling fear of staring into the abyss, but I knew someone had to say it, and I knew that it was me that needed to do it, as there wasn't really anyone else who would be in a position to question her strong will and her determination. I didn't want to burst her bubble, but I knew if she carried on the road would only get harder. Since she was seven years old she had been adamant she would be an actor, and that was the star she had set her course on.

Somehow I felt that maybe by suggesting there might be another route, I might have been putting a reef in front of her to scuttle her ship on, while really I wanted to be her lighthouse. Somehow as a mother there are times you have to be the person that shows them the truth. You have to hold up the mirror and show your darlings that the world does not always bring fairy tale endings and celebrity parties, but I would rather they learned this from me than from someone else. Only someone who loved Charlotte very much could ask that question.

Watching her now, I realise it is what she needed, as her destiny, or her dharma as some might say, will take her further than that, if she can only learn to step out from that place of fear, and into her full power. I can only watch and wait for her to find a place where she will be loved and nurtured, and encouraged to thrive again, because I know it will come to her one day soon. For ultimately, when all is said and done, all you can do is set their little boats to sail on the river of life and trust that they will arrive in one piece, while you watch the breeze take them and carry them away.

Ninety Three

21st January 2008

Dear Mum,

I had a really good session at Psychic School this week where we looked at our fears, and how they really disable us. I worked out I have a double fear – a fear of success and a fear of failure, which might manifest itself as a part that needs integrating in NLP. Parts happen when you have a conflict going on that your unconscious mind can't work out how to solve, so it literally splits off a part of you, and then the various parts have a hard time battling for control.

We also looked again at the nature of inspiration and why it is so important. That to inspire is to be in spirit, to resonate with divinity or your spirit and not your ego. That thoughts can be tamed, and that it is not the event itself that causes the problems, but the meaning you give to that event. As the old saying goes, "It is not the snakebite that kills you but the poison that is left behind." It was one of those sessions that pulled together everything I am learning all over, and knitted the loose ends together, so I can see where each part comes into focus and fits together with all the other parts. We also looked at the nature of negativity, and how it brings your energy down, and how our society is built around reminding us of our fears at every opportunity, particularly in marketing. We are told that if we buy this shampoo, it will solve all our problems, or if you buy this unnecessary plastic object (as Ann always calls them) then you will be happy and fill the gap in your soul that has been niggling at you and wanting to be filled. The thing is, fashion won't fill it, and neither will emotional spending, even if that emotional spending tends more towards the spiritual than the fashionable. As Ann and I have discovered, you can have unnecessary shiny spiritual objects as well as unnecessary plastic ones.

Our teacher also said you have to move forward in baby steps, one at a time, but once you have opened your eyes, you will never go back.

In worse news, the beautiful locust trees that lined my road were cut down today. I was gutted, absolutely gutted. They were so pretty, and then just for one week in June they had the most beautifully scented blossom that would bloom and smell like jasmine under the full moon. All that is left are these sad little stumps and a few giveaway patches of sawdust.

It makes me feel really sad.

Love,
XX

Ninety Four

10th March, 2008

Dear Mum,

I got to Psychic School early tonight, and was really shocked as the teacher asked me if I would like to come back and do the advanced course! I asked for a week to think about it, and then wrote my name on the list halfway through the class. I do still sit there feeling like a fraud, and wondering when someone is going to work out that I shouldn't be there, and yet tonight I realised half the class feels that way too. It is funny how we all put on this front to the world, and hope they wont see how vulnerable we are underneath it all, and yet we are all vulnerable.

I see this course as an exploration of sorts, just a way of seeing what the world looks like through a different lens, but in some ways it also feels like a really important part of my studies. Even if I never do a reading for another human being, just having access to that knowledge is so helpful.

I think it is not as black and white as I thought before though. In the past I used to think that just because I haven't seen dead people from an early age that I have no skill in that area, and yet our teacher says we all have it, it is just a case of practicing and developing. It is a muscle like any other. Just as if I don't go to the gym I don't develop muscles, and if I don't pick up a pen and paper I won't write a novel, if you don't practice this, you don't develop it.

It made me want to just assess the things I have learned so far on this course of studies and the other areas as well, from all my lovely teachers. So far I have learned,

That I don't have to be an emotional sponge unless I choose to be.

That a life lived in fear is not a life really lived.

To trust my feelings, because 99% of the time they are there for a reason.

That the only person who has held me back in life is me. I can be anything I choose to be.

That all roads lead to this one (i.e. you can't be on the wrong path).

That the world is indeed full of magic.

That it is ok to not know the answer to something, just as long as you say you don't know.

To keep asking questions. Always.

Ask for what you really want and it will be yours, and the only person who can stop you is yourself and your own unconscious mind (by blocking you.)

Trust the gods / God / Spirit / Universe or whatever name you want to give it. You are not alone.

The list goes on really. I think my psychic school teacher is the kind of teacher who does things quite quietly and you learn things without realising it half the time.

Well, the next course will be an interesting one. And I guess I need to trust it, and trust me, and stop doubting myself.

Love,
XX

Ninety Five

Dear Mum,

I went to an interesting exhibition today with a friend of mine. It was at the Wellcome Institute, and it was called "Life Before Death." It was a series of photographs of people who were suffering from terminal illness before and after death.

The exhibition was stunning, and I am glad someone is working to demystify the process of dying, as it really is something our society is so divorced from, from the deaths of our loved ones, to our own death, right down to the death of our food. Our food arrives in nice shrink-wrapped packages and doesn't resemble the animal it was once a living and breathing part of.

It is as if we can't deal with the idea of our own mortality, so we pretend it isn't going to happen.

It reminds me that you never shied away from it when you were alive. You often talked about when you would die, or pop your clogs, or kick the bucket or croak, as you so eloquently put it. The truth is you didn't make this a dirty word that we couldn't talk about.

The exhibition reminded me how peaceful most people looked when they have died peacefully. That the ones that were angry about dying and couldn't accept it were fighting a fruitless and pointless battle, in the end, because did they really think they would win? That in accepting our own death and our own mortality we at least have the option of slipping away peacefully, with love and with dignity.

I am not saying we shouldn't give up the fight to live at the first hurdle, but when you can't possibly do anything about it, when your death is coming and you can't possibly avoid it, what is the point in making your own existence so frustratingly difficult? What is the point in the anger? The only person it really hurts is you.

When my time comes, I hope I can approach it with as much dignity and grace as you did.

Love,
XX

Ninety Six

20th June 2008

Dear Mum,

My back has been bad for the last week or so. What
started as a feeling of having been kicked in the kidneys
about a week ago has now escalated into the full muscle
spasms. I haven't been to see the Osteopath as last time I
went I came away with sciatica, so instead I have forgone my
usual gym routine and have been swimming every day
instead, which is quite apt as I am working on "Water Week"
with Denise Linn, where you look at emotional clearing. Last
night I got to the gym at 5.20 in the afternoon and the pool
was empty. I did an initial lap of wild abandon, kicking and
splashing as much as I could in glee, and then gradually
slowed it right down until I was left floating, suspended in
time on my back. It was blissful, having all my senses except
sight and touch dimmed by the water around me. The sounds
of stillness were so soothing, and then through the water I
heard the clunk clunk of the underground trains running
beneath the basement pool.

I have really enjoyed communing with the water there, and
the pool reminds me of an underground grotto, light
reflecting off the ripples in the water, and dancing on the
white ceiling, the ripple and flow of the water as I swim
through it. It is one of the places I can touch the elements
when I can't get home to the moor.

It also struck me as how different it was last night,
compared to the days after you had just gone, when I used to
come to the pool as it was the one place I could cry freely
without anyone being able to tell, as my tears would merge

with the splash of water and remain undetected. (Or so I thought; I could have been seen as the mad crying lady for all I knew.) I don't think I stopped crying for a moment in those early months.

Love,
XX

Ninety Seven: Violet

Each generation has its own challenges. For my generation the challenges were very immediate, such as how to find enough food to feed ourselves, or how to be able to afford medical care (in the years before the Welfare State came into being.) Margaret's generation was different again, and the caring that people were entitled to became even more important, because the close ties to family were slowly dissolving with each generation. Families no longer all lived in the same house like they did before, but spread out across the country, and as they did so, while this brought freedom for some, the support systems that had naturally existed in previous generations also dissolved.

While I was growing up times were definitely hard, but I don't think for one minute that Margaret's generation had it easy, or that Charlotte's generation had it even easier still. The challenges change, but the task is still the same; to spend your time in the physical life to the best of your ability, and to learn the things you wish to learn as well as you can. And to find whatever level of inner peace you can find wherever you are. To try and live to reach your potential in whatever is your own particular path.

For some people this peace comes from helping others, and for some it comes in creative endeavours. For others still it comes in wandering the globe and seeing as much variety as they can, and experiencing as many different forms of life that they can.

When I married Margaret's father, some of my family frowned upon our union. He was then a conductor on the trams, which meant that he was of a lower social class than my family. I thought this was all poppycock; Jim was the kindest man you could ever meet, and he had a heart of gold. I loved him more than I would have ever loved anyone else, and even if that meant we had less money in our household than I may have been accustomed to, I would much rather live in a home that was filled with love than one that was filled with material goods. We may have had to make do sometimes, and we may not have had all the material items a young couple of Charlotte's generation might expect, but I knew none of that mattered, and I was determined to follow my own path, and stay with Jim whatever happened. That is not to say we were always perfectly happy; I had a formidable temper, and poor dear Jim caught the tail end of it sometimes, but his strength lay in the fact that he always loved people as they were, and didn't try to change them.

When Margaret came, I like to think she took the best of both of us; her father's compassionate heart, and my steely determination. This made her a true gift to the world; a worthy challenger of the worst parts of society, and worthy advocate of the most vulnerable parts. My little maid, my star-child.

I like to think about the fact that however small we may think our lives are, and however insignificant we fear they may be, each life creates a ripple that will be felt for generations to come. Our real gift is the effect we can have on others; which can come in many guises; through our children, or the effects of those decisions we make that we think are so fleeting, so momentary. If we can each make just one other life more bearable, more enjoyable, or happier, then we have not lived a life in vain. In truth no life is ever lived in vain, as there is always a way in which each life moved humankind onwards with one step after another. When I look at my Margaret and the immense waves and ripples she alone created, I feel a sense of awe at how much of the world I changed, just by insisting I had to be with her father. How magical the world is, what a wonderful opportunity when you go to the physical plane! One seemingly tiny choice can change generations of people to come.

Sometimes I wonder if the world would be a happier place if more people understood their purpose and the impact they will have on the world, but then to interfere in the natural process of development and evolution would not be helpful. Just like that poor brown butterfly, something in the emotional challenges and the contrasts we live in our lives will always help us to grow and learn, so there is value in every experience. And who am I to judge what other people need? They can ask for help and it will come, but maybe for some people their path is to experience challenge and adversity, and to do it alone. That is not to say we must subscribe to the old Victorian values that tell us everything is god's will and you must wait for your reward in heaven, but sometimes we try to control too much in life and forget to just drift with the current.

The truth is that the world is a far more complex and beautiful thing than we will ever be aware of while we are physical. Once you are able to step beyond the physical and embrace pure energy, then you will see it for what it is.

I look forward to each new person that joins us here, as feeling the bewilderment and awe as they come to realise the truth of their physical existence is so rewarding and such a beautiful thing. It is like watching beautiful flowers uncurl themselves in the sunshine and release their sweet perfume to the world.

Ninety Eight

24th June 2008

Dear Mum,

All change again. I am going back into the extra spin cycle with no fabric softener.

The structure of things at work is changing in a big way, and I am not sure it is in a way I would necessarily have chosen, but I know it is not up to me, and that perhaps sometimes these things come to teach us something new and all I can do is try and remain open to change and be as flexible as I can be. Added to this, my Psychic school teacher is moving to America at the end of the next term, so that must come to an end too.

I know everything has to change and come to an end sometime, but I still feel a little sad and a bit nervous at the coming changes. If I could let go of that fear and just have a bit of a push up on the ladder from someone I would be really grateful. Tonight at psychic school, my reading talked about someone standing in the wings and waiting to help me, but I have been giving the universe the message that it needs to wait as I am not ready yet. I have felt changes brewing in the water for some time, but so far they have been kind, and I haven't needed the tears and tantrums that some of my nemeses have needed to herald new changes. Hopefully I will be able to adapt to the changes with grace, and I will hold myself to that statement later if need be!

I feel a dramatic shift is now coming; the continents are moving and colliding. It is as if all the studying I have done since you left has been to prepare me for the next leg of the journey. I am ready. Bring it on! (and give me a poke in the ribs if I try and back-peddle into my security blanket later!)

Love,
XX

Ninety Nine

19th July 2008

Dear Mum,

A funny old week, with highs and lows. I feel a bit thinly stretched at the moment, which makes it harder to keep on an even keel, added to which I am bone-achingly tired at the moment.

I had a lovely weekend down at home with Ann last week, we were all on our own and it was lovely. We did lots of work. Ann helped me to plan my lesson (I am teaching at the bookshop next week!) and then we had a lovely Saturday night at our neighbours' concert in the village hall. It was magic, and it reminded me again of all the things I miss about being there.

Psychic school as usual was great fun. We are doing readings for guinea pigs every other week (well, human guinea pigs anyway!) I had a really tricky one this week, as a lady came in who was absolutely intent on asking about her love life. She was asking me when her "twin flame" was going to come, and why hasn't he come yet when she has been waiting all this time and as she is nearly forty he needs to get a wriggle on. I suppressed the urge to tell her twin flames don't exist and if they do that he is probably scared to death by her insistence that it is time he got here.

Then the next day I was teaching my class at the bookshop, it was the first in a series, and it was my turn to lead. It felt strange having the tables turned a little so that the pupil is now teaching. All of the changes that are coming seem to be leading me towards growing into myself more. Even in our spiritual group we are now talking about progressing onto the next level. Perhaps it is time for me to grow up at last?

All of these things are contributing to me realising how much I have learned over the last ten years, since I stepped onto the spiritual path. It has been a long and winding one, but I wouldn't swap it for the world.

I am also starting to get excited about holidays. This year Ann and Mary are going to Greece to have their retreat month, so instead of going with them I have persuaded Raven to come to Egypt with me. I feel as if all those things I have been longing for over so many years need to start coming now, so instead of saying "I wish I could go back to Egypt" (which if you remember I have been saying since I was fourteen!) I will actually do it this year.

Love,
XX

One Hundred: Margaret

Lovey,

One of the few things I did regret with the ending of my life was that you and Ann both felt that you wished we had more time together. I know it was the right time for me to go, and we could never argue with Nature, but I know that is sometimes hard for you both to accept. I know in the last days we spent a lot of time talking and I am glad I managed to tell you both just how proud I was (and continue to be) of you all, and just how lucky I was to have loved you and spent my time with you.

There is one thing I keep thinking about since I left you and embarked on my journey here; if I could give you one page of instructions as to how to make the most of your time in the physical life, what would be on it? I know I always said it was not my place to tell you how to live your life, but I think this is somehow different. It is more a list of traveller's tips, like the log books we used to read on those sailing holidays we used to go on, tips from the travellers who had come before, on where to go, and who to see (and which people to watch out for!)

So, if I were to send you this list, I think I would tell you the following.

Do stop giving yourself a hard time – it is really not worth the anguish. Be kind to yourself, and try to see yourself as the people who love you see you.

Don't give energy to those who don't give you the same in return. People don't mean to be unkind, but sometimes they are too focussed on their own world, to see the value of what you have offered them. Don't fret, just allow them space, and take yours too.

People always deserve a second chance in life, don't write people off, but it is not your responsibility to change them, they have to want to change themselves. Give people a break if you can, help match them up to the opportunities you know of, but ultimately then it is their journey to take, and their work, not yours, to make the change happen.

Love freely, and with all of your heart.

Find what inspires you and keep hold of it. Do whatever it is as often as you can, and don't worry about if it pays enough, or if other people can see the value in what you are doing. The rest of the world will catch up with you eventually.

Your NLP teachers are right – people are not bad, they are just doing the best they can with the information they have available to them, and sometimes that doesn't match the information that you have. What one person does may make no sense to you, but unless you have lived inside their skin, don't judge them for it. On their side of the world what they are doing makes perfect sense. Never judge people, as it is a waste of your energy and ultimately it hurts you more than anyone else as it makes you wallow in those bad feelings. Rise above it as often as you can. Remember what your NLP teacher taught you – when you point the finger there are three other fingers pointing right back at you, and they all belong to you!

Don't tolerate unkindness, it is beneath you. That means unkindness to you, or to other people. It will never do you justice to allow someone to take advantage of you.

Learn as much as you can – it is never wasted. One day those skills will come in handy, even if you think it is slightly obscure. If it interests you, then learn about it. It raises your energy if nothing else, which means it is entirely worthwhile.

Also share your learning as much as you can. If people want to know what you know, then help them to learn it as well.

Listen closely to your teachers, but remember to ask questions. They are human too, and bring with them all the contradictions and imperfections that brings.

Remember, imperfection is what makes people beautiful. It gives you a glimpse of their soul, and makes each person unique. Human frailty is what makes them so easy to love, as it is a glimpse of our own divinity. I know that contradicts what other faiths may tell you about God being perfect, but you will see what I mean later on.

Have fun, and laugh as often as you can. Be silly, don't act your age, and dance around the kitchen as often as you can. We were a magical, musical household, as for just those few moments when we laughed so hard the tears ran down our faces as we danced around the kitchen to Gerry Rafferty, we were truly free.

People will always deserve your compassion. But that doesn't mean you have to wear their problems as if they were your own. You can't help people to help themselves if you blur the boundaries between their troubles and yours.

Spend time in nature as often as you can. When you stand on top of a tor with the wind making your eyes water, and your hair whipping around your face; when you float on your back in a warm sea; when you start to see the tiny green buds of leaves start to uncurl themselves on the trees in late March, and when you see a carpet of purple and white crocuses open up from the earth, you will be able to keep life and all of its troubles in perspective.

Remember to find that stillness in life. For just a few minutes each day stop thinking and just be.

If you can find that stillness, remember I am always with you. If you take that time to be still, you may even find you can feel me, curling around you like cool air, warming your skin like the sun. I am with you always.

Much love,

Mum
XX

One Hundred and One

13th October 2008

Dear Mum,

How exciting is this? I am on a plane to Luxor! Do you remember how I was always so fascinated with Egypt when I was a little girl, and I always desperately wanted to go to Luxor to see the great temples and the Valley of the Kings? Well, I think losing you so suddenly made me realise that life is so very short, we need to grasp the opportunities when and wherever they come from.

The journey here has felt like an epic one, and I don't just mean the flight; now I have a sense of a whole new world opening up. The plane has flown down through Europe, and across Greece which I have always loved so much and visited so many times, but this time I am going further. Over the expanse of the Mediterranean, first dotted with islands and the white flecks of the choppy sea below, and then just deep intense blue. Somewhere down there right now, Ann and Mary are sitting on a beach in Kephalonia beneath the black mountain, looking at the sea stretching out to the horizon.

As we flew over the sea and hit the coast of North Africa, the change in continent was marked by the deep intense red colour of the earth, barren and stretching out as far as the eye can see, peppered by small but perfectly laid out buildings, clustered together like little mosaic tiles.

The earth then became desert, and the sands looked a lot like ice flows, the sand flowing in lines like water, and then suddenly I became aware of a strip of intense deep green cutting through the desert. It was the Nile, Mum, and I have to say it is the most beautiful thing I have ever seen. However barren the desert looks, there is always that one strip of fertile green leading us south towards Luxor.

I wish you could see it, and yet I suspect that you are with me. I feel excited for the first time in a long time. Only twenty minutes until we land and I finally get to see my heart's desire for the first time.

Be with me Mumsie, come and tramp round the temples with me. It will be lovely, and what an adventure!

Lots of love,
XX

One Hundred and Two: Violet

If only Charlotte were aware of the true extent of the adventure opening up before her, she would probably feel quite daunted. But then that is why it is good not to see into the future. If we could see what was coming, we might be afraid of grasping what is in front of us with both hands. As the great philosopher Soren Kierkegaard once said, life has to be lived in a forward direction, and yet it is best understood by looking backwards. If we were able to look ahead, the picture we would see would make little sense. Shapes become blurred, and patterns are barely distinguishable through the fog that stops us from looking too far ahead. And yet on this side of the veil, time is not linear. The straight line from past to future is an illusion, and yet it is an illusion that needs to be maintained during the physical time. Because if you knew what was coming, where would the fun be in that? It would be like skipping to the last page in a book, although I must confess I used to do that a lot in my physical youth.

Charlotte is about to embark on the adventure of a lifetime, where all she can do is feel her way into the future; her only map is faded and illegible, her only compass is her heart and that "knowing" feeling it gives her in her stomach. But from our perspective, how exciting it is to watch it all unfold.

As ever, we will be with her. This is the stuff of fairy tales, of stories told to little children gathered at the knee of their grandmother, desperate to hear the tale one more time,

"Grandma, tell us again how you met Granddad, tell us again!"

But it was there on that plane that the story began.

One Hundred and Three

14th October 2008

Dear Mum,

This morning I have awoken with the birds, long before the sun shows any signs of stirring. There is a cacophony of bird chatter coming from the trees on the banks of the Nile. The air is warm, even though it is still dark.

I am excited, because this morning I am to visit Hatshepsut at her temple, and you know how long I have been an admirer of hers. The forgotten King; the lady who strapped on a false beard, and dared to declare herself to be a Pharaoh, and a daughter of the gods, whose name and image was chiselled off the temple walls in an attempt to silence her for all eternity. In fact, I was so excited this morning, I awoke half an hour before our 5am alarm, and was feeling decidedly chirpy, which you will remember is a miracle in itself. Think of all those mornings you struggled to get me out of bed in time for school, there was certainly no reluctance this morning.

Hatshepsut was part of the reason I wanted to come here, so how amazing that we are both here and will meet face to face today.

Much love,
XX

One Hundred and Four

14th October 2008

Dear Mum,

I think I will be writing you lots of letters here. I feel so energised already, and it is only day one. I have indeed plugged myself directly into the mains now, and when I walk past a mirror, I am surprised not to see my hair standing on end and soot marks on my face.

The banks of the Nile look just as I imagined them to, so much so, I have a burning inside which says the banks of the Nile look just as I remembered they would; they are relatively unchanged. The lush green grasses that lead up to the waterside, grazed by goats and played upon by small children. Behind them the fields of sugarcane are tended by hand, except for the occasional chug of the diesel engine which pumps the water for irrigation. So much of me says that I have been here before, the palm trees, the white fisher bird, and behind all of it, the golden mountains and the blue sky.

We are sailing now for Edfu. I say "sail" and yet the engines are loud and vibrate through the whole of the boat, shaking us into our first siesta. Raven is sleeping now, and I am taking a moment to sit in our window, which overlooks the river, and I am feeling a real sense of peace which is underpinned by absolute amazement that I am finally here.

This morning, we left the boat at seven o'clock, and Ahmed, (our guide whom we met last night on arrival) took me by surprise. I knew we were going to the mortuary temple of Hatshepsut, but as we got into our mini bus and started the drive through Luxor, Ahmed switched on his microphone and announced that we were now off to see the Valley of the Kings. I must confess I burst into tears! I have spent so many years imagining this trip, and so many years reading the books and looking at the pictures, and yet before we came here, I deliberately decided not to worry about what our itinerary was, beyond the initial checks when we booked to make sure it took in all the places I wanted to see. So I sat in the back of the bus this morning, hiding behind my sunglasses and hoping no one would notice the mad English woman sitting in the back seat, silently howling with joy at being here.

I can now say that I have stood inside the burial chamber of Tutankhamen, I have gazed upon the paintings on the temple walls, I have looked at his sleeping face, now at peace, as he lies tucked beneath a sheet of simple cotton, his toes poking out of one end, as if he suffered from the same toe-claustrophobia as you and I.

From there we went to Tutmoses III, Seti I and KV2. Ramses IV rested beneath a starry sky in a giant granite sarcophagus, whilst the walls were lined with paintings of Osiris, Isis, and the jackal-headed Anubis.

Ahmed kept embarrassing us at first, as he kept walking us to the front of every long queue. By the third time I no longer cared, and ignored the curses thrown our way in German, French and English.

"It is too hot to queue," he simply said, marching past another line of cursing Europeans.

The heat was already searing when we left the western valley of the dead, and journeyed to see Hatshepsut. I have gazed at her hallowed walls in awe and wonder, and been told her story; how she donned the false beard and named herself King, Pharaoh of Upper and Lower Egypt, and daughter of Amun Ra and Hathor. There are gaps in her story, where Tutmoses III chiselled her likeness from the temple walls. And yet her monument still stands in her name, still we go there to see the space where her name was once uttered, and once more we speak her name with awe and wonder.

From there we went to an alabaster factory, and were shown the process of how the pieces are hand-crafted. I came away with an Isis whose wings form a protective boat, the safety within, my own ship of death.

There! A whole week's worth of experiences, all wrapped up into one morning, and so many more to come. We have opted for an extra trip to Abu Simbel, to see the temple of Ramses the Great, as I couldn't bear to come here and not see it.

I can't help but wonder, which of the great dynasties it was that I lived under, for it becomes ever clearer to me now, that I have walked this land before. And although Islam is now the main religion here, and the god that is worshipped is one God alone. How lonely he seems to be without his brothers and sisters, rivals and friends; alone and solitary. But I suspect that the old gods still stalk this land as they did before, although not all those people who come here are aware of their presence. They think they are dead, when really they just snooze, with one eye open.

Much love,
XX

One Hundred and Five

15th October 2008

Dear Mum,

Tonight we are in Aswan. Today we began in Edfu, and got loaded into horse carriages to drive to the Temple of Horus. The poor horses were very skinny and very sad looking. I had to blank those feelings out a bit, as here it is a bit more complicated. I am aware we are in Africa now, and things may work differently here, but still I wanted to give the horses a good meal, and give them a kind word for all their hard work.

The temple of Horus was truly spectacular. Its walls are very high, and it is from a much later time in history as it was built by the Ptolomies, which I am sure you will remember from your history lessons means it was built in the time of the last dynasty of Pharoahs before Roman rule took over completely, Cleopatra being the last Ptolomy to rule Egypt. The carvings on the temple walls are so huge, it is absolutely stunning, but it filled up with people very quickly. As you know, I have always hated crowds, but today I told myself that the crowds were perfectly normal, as it would have been like that in its heyday anyway; the crush of the people, the smells, the noise, the pushing. Instead of my usual claustrophobia, I managed to maintain a sense of excitement and awe. At one point, we got to the Holy of Holies to take photos, and there was such a crush to get in to see it. People were pushing and shoving and getting very irate, and yet squeezed in to the front and hidden behind the wall of bodies, was a man in a wheelchair. It got quite heated in there, and in the end, Ahmed had to come and rescue us.

I found the strangest thing, when I played back the photos, they are full of light orbs, absolutely loads of them, more than I have ever seen in one place before, which reminds me of my teacher's theory that light orbs are spirits of people who have passed on. It was really stunning, and yet Raven's film doesn't show a single orb.

The scale of everything was just amazing, and everywhere we go, we see little patches of colour that hint at what the temples would have looked like in the past, all brightly coloured and vibrant, just like the Greek temples.

From Horus at Edfu, we returned to the boat, and sailed on up river to Kom Ombo Temple, which stands on a small incline above the place where we moored. This temple was jointly dedicated to Horus, and Sobek, the crocodile headed god.

The temple at Edfu had sustained quite a lot of damage, as had Kom Ombo as a result of being flooded by the Nile every year. They both have heavy silt damage, especially at Edfu where it had been under water for four hundred years, yet it still stands, and it is still beautiful and awe-inspiring and deeply, deeply moving.

Much love from an awe-inspired daughter,
XX

One Hundred and Six

16th October 2008

Dear Mum,

Last night when we sailed into Aswan, the city was all lit up in the dark, and it was beautiful. We went ashore and walked through the Souk, and I loved the sights and the smells, the herb shops and the people, the bright colours everywhere, the fascination of people-watching in a completely different culture.

Today we were up early again to catch the best part of the day, and we visited the Aswan dam, and the unfinished obelisk of Hatshepsut. It was an obelisk which developed a flaw part way through being made, so the workmen left it where it was, which has helped Egyptologists to work out how these things were carved out of the solid granite. They are so huge, it makes me really amazed to think that they were carved by hand, and moved by human muscle and brain. The scientists think that it was finally freed from the rock around it by a system of wooded pegs which were then covered in water or oil to make them expand, thereby cracking the rock. One more we have another example of how a seemingly soft element like water has the power to break rock, just like Lao Tsu pointed out.

Then we sat and drank tea with Ahmed before moving on. I am aware he has been very chivalrous to Raven and I, and I like him very much. He called me his fellow Egyptologist today, and I couldn't help but blush like a child. I am also aware everywhere we go I follow him around with a notebook, taking careful details of the stories he tells us. I probably look even more mad as a result, but hey ho!

Once we had finished our tea, we moved on to the banks of Lake Nasser, and climbed into a boat to travel to Philae, which is the most stunning of all the sites I have seen so far. As the temple on its little island came into view, I must confess I cried again. It was so beautiful; there are lush green bushes and trees dotted around the island, and everywhere you look it is thick with flowers. The island was landscaped to replicate the original island of Philae nearby. This was another temple that was physically moved when Lake Nasser was created; it was literally moved stone by stone in the 1970s as it had continually been flooded and was underwater most of the time. I saw paintings of the island submerged, and people having to visit the temple in a boat that went around the outside.

The temple was just as busy as some of the others we have visited, but the feeling here was very different. Horus at Edfu was quite assertive, vibrant and almost disconcerting. By contrast Isis, Hathor and Horus at Philae were gentle and very soothing. I felt as if I had come home to my mother, and would be safe and nurtured. I got a warm, safe sense from the walls when I touched them, and while some of the people were pushy, they did not get through my defences.

What was strange was that as we looked around and Ahmed told us where things had been, such as the herb gardens, and the sacred fountains, I knew before he pointed them out what would have been where.

Before we came, my dear teacher had said to me that when she visited she had taken a copy of the Hymns to Isis with her and read them aloud, and how magical it had been to hear the words resonate once more within the temple walls. This morning, I had duly packed up my copy of the Hymns to Isis, but had somehow not found the privacy I wanted to read them aloud.

I really did not want to leave, but as I made my way back to the boat with our little group, I took the hymns out from my rucksack to at least read them silently to myself while I was still inside the temple, and Ahmed grabbed them out of my hand and started to read them aloud.

> *"The great Sun God Re speaks:*
> *The King of the Horus Falcons*
> *The Great God*
> *The honoured and foremost*
> *To his beloved son*
> *The great Horus*
> *The Son of Osiris*
> *I am the God*
> *The young soul of Osiris*
> *Who fills the whole land*
> *With the good power of the God's Mother*
> *I am Horus*
> *Who shows himself in glory*
> *On the throne of his father*
> *I am the lord*
> *Over the Nine Gods."* [3]

This somehow seemed so fitting, to have it read so beautifully. I think he is quite exquisite.

As we sailed away I felt very sad.

Tomorrow we must awake at two in the morning to travel to Abu Simbel.

Love,
XX

One Hundred and Seven: Margaret

Dear One,

Some of my friends felt that they gave up their lives when they had children. I never did, I felt that you and your brother and sister all added to my life; my lovely babies, who grew into such beautiful adults. I always felt so proud of you all, and in my last days was so thankful for you.

By choosing to have you, I inevitably put some aspects of my life on hold, and that was my choice. In my day as a young Mum, a career was almost unheard of, and I wouldn't have had it any other way. Once you had all grown up and were independent, I relished the new role my career gave me. I loved the challenges, the learning, and the opportunities to help so many people. Yet I know in my final days, it was not my career that I reflected on. Of course, I was pleased with it as an achievement, but in the end there were so many things that were so much more important and precious to me.

So my lovely, whilst I did not sacrifice anything for you, I don't want you to sacrifice anything for my passing either. Life must go on, and now that I am watching you beginning to really live your life again, I know you will be fine. I want you to really listen to your heart now. What does it say to you? I always meant it when I said that I didn't mind what job you did, or what kind of life you lead; I just want you to be happy.

In the last few years before my passing, I know you were sometimes unhappy. You talked to me often of the grey zone that you felt your life had become, and I could see on your face that the ache in your heart wasn't nurtured by your relationship any more, even if you were not ready to see it. I saw your deep loneliness, even when you didn't.

If you can take anything good from my passing, my dearest one, my special girl, please take every opportunity you have to grasp joy with both hands and live for the moment. Love yourself as kindly as you give your love to others and find all of the things you can that feed your soul and make you feel alive and good.

Love, as always,

Mum

One Hundred and Eight

20th February 2011

Dear Mum,

It has been so long since I wrote to you last, I am not sure where to begin. Should I fill you in on the events since my last letter, or should I assume you know what has been happening here? I think that is one area of etiquette Debrett's couldn't help me with...

Well, needless to say I did come back from Egypt, after several rather hair-raising adventures! I like to think you would have been proud of me for those, and perhaps may have been cheering me on from the sidelines. Ahmed and I married in Cairo several months later, and although I had hoped we could do it on your birthday, the embassy was shut that day as it was the holidays, so instead we married on Granddad's birthday. That was nearly two years ago now.

This week we have been watching some very different scenes unfolding in Cairo, but while a Revolution has unfolded in Tahrir Square, just round the corner from where we always stay when we go to there, we have watched it from the safety of the News Channel, for now we are back in London, and it is now Ahmed's turn to have a big adventure.

I finally got to sign up for my Masters Dgree course, with Ahmed's help, and I am now a University student! The course is wonderful, so inspiring, and I relish every moment there. We had a few dramas trying to get me onto the course, as life has been quite hard work for a couple of years. It seems that starting a life together is quite a challenge when you have nothing to start with, but finally things are beginning to settle, and while we don't yet have a fairytale ending (if anyone *ever* does) we are both very happy, and working hard to get to a place where we can both feel we are doing something we love. We laugh a lot, we write messages to you on helium balloons on Mother's Day and watch them soar up into the sky, wondering if they will reach you. We also dance around the kitchen when we listen to Arabic music, and talk of you often, even though you and Ahmed never met. It is a household which laughs and cries, has occasional tears and tantrums, and is very much about living our lives as much as we can to the full.

When I was starting to study again, I couldn't help but draw so many parallels with the time that you went back to University as a mature student too. The challenges of finding funding or a way of paying for the course, the challenge of thinking you must be the only duffer in a class of intellectuals, and the recurring question of "who do I think I am, imagining I could be an Masters student?" Dad was able to remind me that you had all of those same challenges, so I guess you have been the inspiration behind this adventure too, Mumsie, like you have been the inspiration behind many others. I got my first essay back last week and I got a Merit for it, so I can't be all that stupid!

Your life and your death have both changed my life irrevocably, but these days I find myself being more content to just be and not ask too many questions. I am learning because I love learning, not just so I can reach a place where I think I am more clever, or better. I don't need to seek the future anymore because I know it will come in its own good time.

So for now I am learning to take each day as it comes. There are still so many things I would like to do in this lifetime, before I come and find you again, but for now I am content to let each adventure unfold in its own time and in its own way. I am also learning to find peace again. This week I have been thinking about you a lot, as I was on a course that was just down the road from "63" where you used to stay with your special friends when you came to London. Each

241

lunch time I have had a lovely walk in Kensington Gardens, and sat on a bench overlooking the part where the Canada Geese and the swans float gently down the Serpentine. For just those few moments I have sat in silence again and just thought of you, and while I missed you with the same old ache I will always miss you with, I have also wondered what we would talk about as we sit and watch the clouds pass overhead, and what I came up with is this.

We would sit as we always did, and talk of things trivial and important. We would sit and just enjoy each other's company, and the opportunity for just one moment's peace while the world dashes around outside. And while I sat there thinking of you, I could close my eyes and almost feel you sitting right there beside me on the bench.

I remain, as always, your loving daughter,
XX

Acknowledgements

Many adventures were had in the writing of this book, and I was lucky enough to have some very special people who guided me along the way.

Firstly, as ever, I would like to thank my family for their support in helping me to write this story. It has taken us all on quite a journey, but without the constant reassurance and consultations with both my father and my sister, this book would not exist. Also thanks to Kath for the final letter from Margaret, which was formed from one of her very own conversations. Also thanks to Lizzie Conrad-Hughes and Rebecca Wood for reading the early drafts and teaching me the difference between its and it's!

Secondly, I would like to dedicate this book to my teachers. In the dark times following Mum's departure, my teachers became my lighthouses, shining a little light on the dark areas of my life, holding my hand while I learned to walk again, and encouraging me to take a few leaps of faith. It is to them I owe a huge debt, and one I will probably never get to repay. My few brief words cannot give the full breadth of what they gave me, and without them I would probably not be here, and I know the book wouldn't be. Their names are listed in the dedication, and just in case any readers may wish to look them up, their details are as follows:

Dr Christina Oakley Harrington who runs the beautiful Treadwells Bookshop in Bloomsbury, which is the most exciting and curious bookshop you could ever hope to see. Christina is my longest standing teacher, and has guided me though some very significant rites of passage – www.treadwells-london.com

Dr David Shephard – the exquisite Master Trainer of NLP, Hypnosis and many other things, who gave me the tools to help myself and showed me that the world is indeed a magical place to explore, and that the only thing stopping me from achieving whatever I want is my own unconscious mind –

Also thanks to Sally Davies who coached me and my then grumpy unconscious mind through my training, with much kindness and patience, but also the strength to not take any of my excuses, and not let me believe them either. My unconscious mind and I are much happier together as a result – both lovely people are found at www.performancepartnership.com

Katherine Beattie – my lovely sister, who I am sure will be very surprised to read that I consider her to be one of my teachers. But she is, and is one of the most significant. The things she has taught me are far too vast to list in one small paragraph!

Tomas D'Aradia, a.k.a. Phoenix – master of tarot and photographer extraordinaire, who taught me to stand up and look the death card in the eye, that sometimes there is "death and..." and sometimes there is just death. But that since the tarot deck does not end at the death card there can also be life after death. Also thanks for warning me that Egypt was coming, even if I wasn't ready to hear it yet – www.phoenixphotography.co.uk

Becky Walsh who taught me at the College of Psychic Studies with humour, wisdom, love and deep knowledge, even though I was quite determined to convince myself that my being there was a big mistake. Here I learned how to connect with my own feelings to know what it was I was thinking and feeling around me, whether it was seen or unseen, and my reading lists became much wider – www.beckywalsh.com

Denise Linn – the splendid author of many books, and the host of a weekly radio show, whose wonderful programme Soul Coaching has taught me many things, and helped me to have a good emotional clearout once in a while. She has given me the strength to acknowledge that the soul loves the truth more than the fear of it, and that what you resist persists. I was lucky enough to meet her at a seminar in London, and I am determined that one day my sisters and I will make it to Summerhill Ranch to become Soul Coaches - www.deniselinn.com

Dr Wayne Dyer – my virtual teacher of the Tao who opens my eyes to many wonderful new things on a daily basis, and reminds me that the place for ego-driven thinking is not here and now, and that I don't have to force things to happen – just being is enough – www.drwaynedyer.com

Abraham Hicks, via Esther and Jerry Hicks, whose humour at the prospect of croaking took the sting out of its tail and allowed me to realise that intention is everything, that death is just part of the journey, and it is much kinder to yourself to stop paddling upstream and just go with the flow – www.abraham-hicks.com

Finally, I would like to dedicate this book to my mum, Margaret, and my grandmother, Violet. I am sure I was not alone when I was writing it.

If you have enjoyed this book and would like to find out more, or for more information about my writing, please go to www.rebeccabeattie.co.uk

Feedback is always a wonderful thing, positive or otherwise. Please do get in touch, as I would love to hear from you.

Also, reviews on websites like Amazon are always really important to a writer, as they can really help other people make the decision to read your work, and will encourage the writer to keep writing! If you have loved this book and would like to help others find it, please do leave reviews on Amazon or on Good Reads.

Notes

[1] This was Robin Hobb in her splendid series of books, The Tawny Man trilogy

[2] The words of the Poem shown in italics are taken from "The Ship of Death" by DH Lawrence, published in Last Poems (1932)

[3] These words are taken from the Hymns to Isis, which are inscribed on the temple walls at Philae.

Printed in Great Britain
by Amazon

26453554R10139